Smoke signals

Gerrit Postma

ISBN : 978-0-244-61647-2

Publisher:

Stichting Cosmic Fire Foundation
Continentenlaan 52
9642 BH Veendam
Netherlands

For Candy

My sincere thanks to everybody who assisted in creating this book, by thinking along, proof reading, correcting and last but not least by prodding me till I did this English version.

I

Sometimes a telephone is an essential help, at other times it's a nuisance. At this moment it was supposed to be the latter, since I was supposedly hard at work. I was sitting at my desk punching a future brochure on folklore into my computer, so I ought to have considered the disturbance of my little electronic talking device as an interruption. In reality the booklet was a rather boring routine job, and I was glad to be distracted from finding out if an Easter bonfire was called a Poasboak or a Paosbaok in the Twente dialect.

I said "Wim Versluys" to the thing, because that has been my name for many years and I hate lying, unless it was absolutely necessary, naturally.

"Pater," the contraption replied, possibly influenced by the person at the other side of the in this case wireless line.

Pater was a high ranking somebody at IPOL, an international police cooperation something. We met some time ago when my buddy Eddy and I had a difference of opinion with the Baltic Mafia. That had resulted in quite a bit of spending money for the three of us, including my lucrative government contract to write booklets on folklore, for instance. If you can't control your curiosity and want to learn more I've got some bad news for you, "Waddengoud" in which all is revealed is for now only available in the Dutch language.

"Mister Pater, I thought our fishing trip was planned for next week?"

"Fishing trip" being our code for generating more spending money in an almost legal way.

"You're right, but there is a problem. Mr. Kamminga has disappeared, you know."

I was pleased that for just once I knew something IPOL didn't.

"Eddy is in America, he was invited to look into groundwater pollution."

"In South Dakota, that's correct, but that's where he disappeared."

That shut me up for a moment, and the pleased feeling went downriver fast.

"Can I see you?"

"Naturally, I'd like that. When?"

"Now?"

Something dingdonged in the hallway. I opened the door, and Pater stepped in, past me. He neatly hung his blue gabardine overcoat on a coat hanger, and led the way into the living room. Easy, those self-service visitors.

Pater cast an appreciating eye around the large living room that had been created in what once was the barn section of the former small farmhouse. The ground floor of the original house part was mainly occupied by the offices of my wife, Ria, and myself, and by a book collection that was growing wildly out of control.

"Nice job."

I thanked him for the compliment, and pointed at a comfortable couch that Ria had found at a yellow and blue Swedish furniture store.

"Coffee?"

"Naturally."

A few minutes later I was sitting opposite him. He took a sip, nodded approvingly, and started.

"Some time ago Mr. Kamminga came into contact with a group which is concerned about the quality of drinking water on an Indian reservation in South Dakota. Rightly so, by the way. Kamminga saw a possibility to deploy his tame bacteria."

Eddy was attached to the university in the nearby city. He had developed some interesting methods to let bacteria clean up all kinds of contaminations, in both soil and water. Besides that he also produced some very agreeable alcoholic beverages, but that was purely as hobby.

"He decided to go there on a personal trip. Mrs. Kamminga went along, they wanted to combine the trip with a vacation. We know that Kamminga collaborated for a few weeks with his colleagues over there, but all of a sudden they both disappeared. They just didn't show up at their hotel anymore. That was two weeks ago, and nobody knows what is going on."

I looked him straight in the eye...

"You said "we know", do you mean that you kept an eye on him over there?"

He nodded.

"I'm always interested in people who are of importance to me, with whom I'm cooperating."

Okay, so I wasn't all that paranoid, my feeling of being followed might even be justified.

"Should I be looking for a tracker in my car?"

Sometimes Pater's face has a twitch that might be a distant relative to a smile. Like now.

"Waste of time, you'll never find it."

As soon as I had some spare time I should wonder if I ought to feel flattered, irritated, afraid or especially safe. Anyhow, any illusion of privacy was a now quickly fading memory.

I scratched behind my left ear since the right one was holding a coffee mug.

“Before we push the “general alert” button, couldn’t they have just taken a few days off, just the two of them? Young love and all that, you know.”

Pater sighed.

“I wish that was true. Kamminga had an appointment for which he never showed up, and he didn’t call to cancel. All of their toiletries are still in the bathroom. A laptop was still there, switched on too. As far as we can tell all of their luggage is still there, except for the clothes they were wearing.”

Truth be told, that did sound convincing

“Didn’t their car have a tracker?”

He sighed again.

“It did, but at the last moment at the airport they decided on a different type of car, so they got an unprepared one instead.”

“And now what?”

“I don’t know how much you know about reservations, but my colleagues over there are not overly eager to start an investigation on Indian territory, they have some kind of semi-autonomous status. In spite, or maybe because of that, my friends would not in the least object to you poking around a bit, as a concerned friend. Maybe you’ll learn something, maybe you’ll trigger a reaction.”

“I’m going to America? Did it ever occur to you to ask me first?”

He looked a bit surprised at me.
"Would you have hesitated for even a second?"
"No, but…"
"There you go. Naturally you'll get support, but they will stay out of sight, the federal government is not overly popular over there."
From an inside pocket of his navy blue top quality woolen suit jacket he conjured up a small bundle of papers. He handed me the first one.
"Your ticket. The flight is early in the morning, day after tomorrow."
And a few more.
"Voucher for a rental car. Voucher for a hotel in Rapid City, for your first night over there, since you'll be arriving rather late. Reservations at a bed and breakfast in Porcupine. Kamminga was in a motel in Kyle, so this is neutral territory. Overview of the Kammingas' schedule, and yours. Concise information on the area, I do recommend doing some more research yourself."
He paused for a sip.
"And Ria? What will I tell her?"
Another paper.
"Mrs. Versluys is leaving on Friday for a work meeting in Atlanta, she should be hearing about that right now. This is her ticket from Atlanta to Rapid City a week later for when her meeting there is over. So she can join you."
I look at him with refreshed admiration.
"Is there any pie you don't have a finger in?"
He shrugged.
"I just happen to have a lot of acquaintances at in lot of the right places."

* * *

Ria was literally bouncing with excitement when she came home that evening.

"Hey, I'm going to America!"

After a moment and with great regret I wrestled myself out of her embrace.

"I know, so am I."

She looked at me with mouth agape.

"What do you mean?"

I told her about the coffee visit I had today. She was hesitating between indignation because she wasn't going to America purely on her own merits, and concern for Natasja and Eddy.

"What do you think happened to them?"

To demonstrate I'm perfectly capable of doing several things at the same time, multitasking in other words, I shrugged and pushed one of the microwave's buttons.

"I wish I knew, but I really don't have the faintest idea."

Absentmindedly she watched our rotating dinner, then she gave me a worried look.

"I'd prefer you didn't go, I'm worried something could happen to you as well."

"Thank you, and believe me, I'll be as careful as possible. You know Eddy, there's probably something odd but perfectly innocent behind all this."

Perhaps I'd even believe it myself if I'd repeat it often enough. Ria didn't, by the way. She pulled me against her again. The microwave wanted to have the last word, and pinged to attract our attention.

* * *

Okay, so I had to go to South Dakota. I've been to the US a few times, to New York and as recent as last year to Atlanta, Georgia when Ria had to go there for her work, and we had combined the trip with a short vacation. From this area I knew virtually nothing, except that it probably was situated to the South of North Dakota, but to be honest I wasn't even too sure about that. Our own country's map is more than a little screwed up in that regard as well, our South Flevoland polder is to the southwest of East Flevoland, which of course is to the northeast, though not as far as the North East Polder, and then there is the Western Scheldt River, which is to the south of the more northeastern Scheldt River, besides the point they're both estuaries and not rivers, so that's all a bit out of whack. The information Pater had given me was on the anorexic side of slim. So, I dived into my chips box and fired up Google's boiler. To my surprise I almost immediately found a link to a foundation in my own area, in the town of Veendam, that occupied itself with the Native Americans in the Pine Ridge Reservation – exactly the place where Eddy and Natasja had disappeared.

I dialed the number listed on the website, a woman with an American accent answered. After hearing my explanation she passed me on to a man with a Twente accent, so from the east of the country. Clearly an international organization... Yes, they had some good contacts in the area, and they'd been there themselves. Could I come visit for some more information? Sure just say when.

That "when" was that very afternoon, since it was the last available afternoon before my departure. In the meantime he gave me a link to his personal blog with more pictures of their last trip

Ommelanderveensloot-Tweededwarsdiep – Veendam was, mainly due to the characteristic lack of traffic congestions in the east of our province, Groningen, just a hair under half an hour. I followed the sign to the RDW, the national car registration authority, as instructed, and entered the street across from that office.

I had hardly rested my finger on the door bell when the corresponding door was opened by a less than young person, complete with belly, glasses, beard and suspenders.

"Mr. Versluys? I am Gerrit Postma."

I confirmed my identity and followed him through a hallway filled with cardboard boxes to a living room that was mainly filled with stacks of plastic crates and more cardboard boxes. He saw my surprised look.

"The foundation is running a few web shops, a very important source of income for us. It actually supplies the main part of our income, and it pays for the largest part of our support to the Lakota."

A slim dark blonde lady was sitting in one of the bluegrey rotating chairs, but jumped up when I came in. A dog that was, as far as I could tell, a Scottish collie that had been washed too hot and had shrunken because of that, sniffed my pants leg with great interest.

"Don't pay any attention to me, I was just leaving!"

Postma introduced us, and claimed her was name Ankie Schieving, and that she ran a Buddhist center in neighboring Wildervank.

"There is a Buddhist center in Wildervank?"

Smiling she bared a set of teeth that would never make a dentist any money.

"We're really there, but we're not really well known yet. It is a center for Tibetan Lama Buddhism. My son even became a monk."

While I filed both the card and information she'd given me, slightly surprised to be honest, she said her farewell.

In the meantime another lady had joined us, who introduced herself as Candy Postma, with the accent I had noticed during our phone call.

I was offered the choice of identical rotating chairs, plus coffee. I accepted both gratefully.

While we were waiting for coffee, Postma asked:

"You're a journalist, you mentioned, and you want to write about South Dakota?"

That was indeed the reason I had given for my visit since the search for Eddy and Natasja would have taken a bit too much explaining.

"May I ask where you're planning to stay?"

I checked one of Pater's papers.

"Dancing Pony Trading Post, Porcupine."

They looked at each other.

"Tell Susie hello from us! By the way, that's a postal address, in reality it's closer to Manderson."

That didn't make any difference to me, I had never heard of either place, but just a few days later I wished I had paid more attention to that particular bit of info.

A filing box filled with brochures appeared on the table, and on a laptop a longer series of photos than I had seen on the blog appeared. The Postmas were brimming with useful information, and I was amazed to learn that there were third world like situations in what was supposed to be the richest country on the globe. I noticed that Eddy's polluted drinking water was mentioned, I was advised to stock up on bottled water before entering the reservation. The ground water, and therefore the drinking water, were polluted by naturally appearing uranium, and by chemicals which remained from of the time when the military used parts of the area as a chemical warfare testing ground and bombing range.

My host and hostess' enthusiasm was infectious, the coffee was excellent.

When I took my leave a few hours later I had learned a lot of useful stuff. In my notebook was a long list of email addresses and phone numbers of various eventually handy contacts they knew via their charity work.

Sometimes you just need a bit of luck.

* * *

Once back at home I dived back into my computer, this time armed with both the Pater as well as the Postma info. Now that I knew some more search terms I was soon flooded with information.

In short, one treaty after another were broken by the American government, during the second half of the Nineteenth Century the Lakota Sioux Indians were given a large part of South Dakota as their reservation, including the Black Hills and Badlands, which were considered sacred lands. Immediately after that gold was found in the Black Hills, so that area was taken from them. The Oglala Lakota, a "band" or subdivision led by Red Cloud, got the Pine Ridge reservation. Through a series of slights of hand they ended up with only the worst parts of it.

In 1890 the infamous Wounded Knee massacre took place, when a few hundred unarmed men, women and children were killed by the US Army.

Much more recent, in 1973, Wounded Knee was occupied by activists demanding more rights for Indians and protesting against the reservation administration. That didn't result in immediate concrete results, but it brought to the attention of the world the miserable conditions the Indians were living in, it gave them a lot of self-confidence.

There still is a lot wrong over there, most notably the poverty, but they're allowed to use and teach their own language again, and there are many involved in improving the situation. Sadly it was obvious that this was not a situation that could be fixed overnight.

In the meantime my suitcase was nearly completely packed, all I had to add tomorrow morning were my toiletries. My shoulder bag with camera, documents and everything else I figured I might need during the trip was next to it, all I had to add to that one was my tablet. Phone and tablet were being charged, and I figured I was just about ready for my trip.

Ria didn't have to leave till two days after me, so she was still in the organizing piles of stuff stage.

While messing around and getting organized my mind kept wandering to Eddy and Natasja. What the hell could have happened to them? I decided that if I found out nothing serious was going on I'd puncture their plane's tires so they'd be forced to walk home – that would teach them!

II

A bit of background info for the non-Dutch readers.

My home town of Ommelanderveensloot-Tweededwarsdiep, which really ought to exist outside my chronicler's imagination, is a hamlet, strung out along a disused canal. It's in the north of the Netherlands, in the eastern part of the province of Groningen, an area once known for its peat diggings, and still known as the "peat colonies".

Our national airport, Schiphol, is a bit west of our capital, Amsterdam (not to be confused with The Hague, which is the seat of the government), and therefore a few hours removed from my humble abode.

Ergo I had to leave home at ridiculous o'clock to get to the airport the mandatory few hours before departure. I drove through Frisia, made a left at the Joure roundabout with its gigantic coffee cup, and soon found myself in only light traffic on the highway through Flevoland, a long stretch on average four meters under sea level, but hey, I'm Dutch, we don't really register stuff like that. Via Hilversum to the Amsterdam A10 ring road, and the Schiphol access road.

Pater had arranged for a valet service to take the car off my hands, but probably only because it's cheaper to have them park it several municipalities away than pay the exorbitant airport parking rates, the cheapskate.

Once inside the Schiphol terminal everything ran smoothly. My ESTA (Electronic System for Travel Authorization) declaration, that nowadays takes the place of a visa for us, was still valid from my last trip. Pater had printed my boarding pass already, my API (Advance Passenger Information) form for the American authorities had been filled out by him too, undoubtedly truthfully, because that's the kind of guy he is. Where would we be without forms…? Odd country, the United States, on the one hand they spend tons of money to lure in tourists, on the other hand even more tons to discourage them with a plethora of checks and rules. One would almost not feel welcome after all that circus.

I flew with Delta, but since they're in some kind of alliance with our native KLM, I had to check in there.

There were only a few people ahead of me at the check-in desk. Naturally there was amongst them a lady who had put too much in her suitcase and was now transferring stuff to her carry-on luggage since obviously she didn't want to pay extra for the overage, judging by the stacks of clothing and other things she had surrounded herself with.

Soon my suitcase, after being properly labeled, disappeared per conveyer belt – always a good moment to hope it would indeed arrive at the proper destination, preferably at the same time as myself.

After having passport and boarding pass checked by a border guard I strolled at ease, my shoulder bag – you'll never guess it – over my shoulder – to the departures area. At the ATM which also distributed US dollars upon request there was a sizeable line, but I had plenty of time, even for the overpriced espresso afterwards. The various tax-free shops didn't exactly fascinate me. Neither Ria nor me used perfumes, I never smoked and I wasn't supposed to take alcohol into the reservation, a dry area.

That limited the choice to stuff I didn't want or could get at a much lower price at home.

After a few kilometers of conveyer belts along huge traditional Dutch Delft blue earthenware tiled tulip pots I arrived at the proper gate. There was a good sized line here, naturally caused by the sadly necessary extensive security check of shoes, belts, shoulder bags, contents of pants pockets, etc.

A not extremely young anymore and obviously American couple was in front of me, and told me passionately about their boat trip along various Russian rivers, and they enquired how long I had been in the Netherlands. I assured them I was born and raised here, which caused them to wonder where I was heading. When I told them I was visiting a friend in an Indian reservation they gave me some odd looks. Not a first for that to be honest.

Thoroughly scanned I was allowed to put shoes and belt back on, and I could find a seat in the rapidly filling waiting room.

After a little over half an hour the first passengers were allowed to board the Airbus 330-300, after about five minutes it was my row's turn. I had chosen a window seat since I like to see things on the way, and over the wing, where the various shakes and other moves which planes subject their passengers to are least troubling.

While I was still philosophizing – you didn't know I could do that without booze, did you – about the fact that such a huge hunk of metal, and on top of that stuffed with as many as three hundred people, their luggage and loads of fuel, really ought not be able to fly, when the darn thing proved me wrong by going skywards at an impressive angle.

To be honest that was a good thing, an ocean is a big swim, and I never got my advanced diploma.

Those small things that I had to push into my ears and connected to my arm rest did not produce enough sound to drown out the engine noise, resulting in me not being able to follow the movie on the small monitor in the backrest in front of me. The paperclip-like thing with which I had to attach them onto my ears were not very pleasant at all. I know everybody is watching their pennies, but offering movies without a proper way to hear the sound is nonsense, and I'm being polite here. With a mixture of envy and irritation I watched a fellow across the aisle who had plugged in proper headphones he had brought along, and now probably was able to hear everything. The maroon, to quote the immortal Bugs Bunny. Why did he think of it, and it had slipped my mind since my last flight, when this undoubtedly had irritated me as well. The logical thing was to blame the rush caused by Eddy through Pater. So I switched the monitor to flight information, and saw a small digital airplane projected on an equally digital map of Great Britain. I peered out through the thick Plexiglas, the thick cloud cover below us confirmed the screen's opinion.

Delta took good care of us, but the coffee bearing the slogan "Seattle's Best" only inspired me to torch Seattle at the earliest opportunity.

According to my digital plane the cloud cover over Great Britain had been replaced by the cloud cover over Ireland. The difference was negligible. Actually the difference just wasn't there.

Luckily a friendly flight attendant came around with the first meal of the flight, and to be honest I had been looking forward to it.

By the time we had passed Iceland, which was hiding discretely behind the horizon, according to my by now trusty monitor we still had some 4,500 kilometers or slightly less than six hours of flight ahead of us. Because of the head wind of over 200 kilometers per hour we were doing ‘only’ about 650. Kilometers, of course, I’m Dutch. Outside it was 57 below zero, Celsius of course, I’m Dutch, remember, so I decided not to try if the window opened.

A few 5-star Sudoku’s later my screen reported that we were passing over the Southern point of Greenland. Pure swindle, encouraged by the local tourist bureau – there wasn’t anything green in sight, only ragged grey peaks with a liberal coating of snow.

Newfoundland was equally fake, it didn’t look newly found at all, I think it was there for quite a time already with all those wrinkly rocks and stuff.

It was feeding time, but this time I avoided the coffee-colored water and switched to orange juice. Luckily that didn’t suck.

Somewhere over Canada the flight attendant doled out customs forms. I truthfully declared that I wasn’t bringing any gifts for anybody, and had nothing else of interest to report. I hoped this was the final document for now, and that they believed me.

At least there was now something to see outside while Canada slowly scrolled beneath us. We were still far too high to recognize details, but roads and cities could be separated by the surrounding landscape.

The cabin crew made a few last rounds to deliver water for those who were so inclined and to collect waste paper and other trash. It had been quite a long sit, and I was looking forward to stretching my legs again.

* * *

Do you get a distinct picture in your head when you hear the name Detroit? Neither do I. Naturally I knew it was situated somewhere in the vicinity of one of the Great Lakes, don't ask me which one but it undoubtedly was a very large and very wet one, at a stone's throw from the Canadian border which never threw back any stones, and that it was home to the long-suffering American mobility tins industry, but that was about it. According to the Internet, so it had to be true, the population had fallen in a few years' time from 1.8 million to about 700,000 – not really a recommendation. I had no inclination to see any of this and I didn't have to, I only was there to change planes for my next flight, to Minneapolis.

Okay, that changing planes took a few hours, and just as well. An unknown (to me, at least) number of years ago the airport had to be expanded. Instead of just planting a new pier in the Schiphol way a new terminal for international flights was built in a field a way off, and connected to the main building with a long tunnel. By descending an escalator, going through that long tunnel, and up another escalator I arrived at the main building of the

Edward H. McNamara terminal – and no, I don't have the faintest idea who Ed is or was, and just like you I'm not interested enough to Google it. It seemed that just before my arrival at least one huge plane crammed with Chinese had landed, and all of them were now standing in front of me in a long line through a maze of ribbons between metal posts, in a long undulating line to have our passports checked. Together with my fellow arrivals from Amsterdam we joined the line and slowly we shuffled through the maze, one Chinese at the time. Naturally only two or three of the ten checkpoints were manned.

After I watched the welcome film on the enormous screen on the opposite wall a few dozen times it finally was my turn. My passport was thoroughly checked, I was fingerprinted and my photograph was taken. The good man wanted to know what I was doing in his country, so I told him I was visiting a friend in South Dakota. As far as I knew I was not wanted there nor anywhere else in the US as a result of my previous visits, but after a reception like that I expected nothing less than a few tightly suited FBI-ans appearing next to me to measure me for a black and white striped outfit with a number on it. If they would put a chip in my neck the next time I'd visit it wouldn't really surprise me anymore. It was all a bit ironic considering our proximity to the Canadian border, with more holes in it than the average colander. Perhaps I should consider entering on foot next time?

Nothing and nobody appeared next to me, nobody measured me for anything, and I was allowed to find my suitcase. It obviously was tired of going round and round on the carrousel, and didn't protest at all when I dragged it towards the exit.

Via customs, which didn't want to see or know anything, I ran into an ambush of airport people who were all anxious to find out where I was going. I still had little to hide, so I told them. They compared my statement with my boarding pass and the label the friendly Schiphol lady had attached to my suitcase, found enough corresponding points, and dropped my case on a conveyor belt. And we had been reunited for such a short time …

There wasn't any time for tears, I was referred to TSA, the Transport Security Administration. They were people, as I found out, who wanted to X-Ray me again, after I had put my shoes, belt and shoulder bag in separate plastic trays for further investigation. My tablet obviously was considered such a big threat that it had to be X-Rayed on its own. I presumed my doctor would have received the outcome by the time I returned.

I got scolded for forgetting to take off my watch and was allowed to put on my shoes and belt again. A monitor informed me where I could find my Minneapolis flight. At the top of yet another flight of stairs a gigantic sign welcomed me to Michigan. Nice gesture, but as you know I wasn't really there.

Everything was clearly indicated, and I took a nicely streamlined little red train that took me high along the side of the hall to the area of my gate, it looked like miles away. Just a bit larger and I would have needed a plane just to get to the other end. I had lots of time, but I preferred spending that in the vicinity of my departure point, to prevent any mishaps.

The friendly lady at the gate's desk assured me I was at the right place, but also that the boarding passes Pater printed for me were not legible by the United States equipment. Within moments she had printed two American boarding passes, one for each of the remaining two legs of the trip.

Because the plane was nowhere to be seen yet I reconnoitered the local eateries. Prices were rather high, even for an airport. The banana I had set my mind on cost about as much as I had estimated as the price of the whole island it grew on. Out of desperation I only bought something that I hoped was somehow related to a pizza, and a soft drink. Medium appeared to be half a bucket. Together they made a considerable dent in my pile of local green bills.

I spent my waiting time with one of my favorite occupations: people watching. Airports are ideal locations for that, at few other places can you see that many different types and behaviors. And let’s be honest: America is host to a select assortment of types and behaviors. Hordes of people in the widest differing assortment of outfits and hair styles, carrying the most extreme collection of luggage passed my personal little stage.

Finally my flight was announced. Not totally unexpected, since I had seen the plane being coupled to the sky bridge to unload a horde of Detroit-bound passengers and returning Elsewhere-bounders. Immediately afterwards a new crew went on board, a cleaning crew made their rounds in record time, and supplies were replenished.

This time it was, according to my papers, an Airbus 320, with only space for about half as many passengers as the transatlantic contraption I arrived in.

I found my new seat at my new window, and watched interestedly the comings and goings outside. A herd of vehicles circled the machine to bring all kinds of stuff. I sincerely hoped my suitcase was part of the “stuff”.

We taxied for several miles before the machine took its usual running start and took to the skies. There were only a few clouds around, so I could enjoy the view of lakes and oddly striped fields. The few clouds that were present presented a spectacular view themselves.

The only negative aspect of the whole flight was the dirty water that Delta passed for coffee here as well. Obviously they did feel guilty, because besides a handful of cookies we also got some baggies of peanuts.

No video screen in front of me this time, only the bare rear of a backrest, and the same mail-ordery magazine I leafed through over the Atlantic. Puzzles are only made to keep us off the streets and are therefore senseless occupations, there are other possible brain gymnastics imaginable, so the Sudoku booklet remained in my bag while I kept a fascinated eye on the landscape slowly rolling by beneath us.

It was funny passing over a small airfield, two landing strips at a straight angle to each other. I took a few pics of down below, but I feared that because of the slight haze they might not be extremely successful. The cloud formations were a better and more fascinating subject than the hazy green checkerboards.

* * *

A different color carpeting, a different airport. According to the signs Minneapolis was Siamese twinned with St. Paul, but I was here only to change planes again, so this kind of intimate family relations could not fascinate me now.

Before I deplaned I had a pleasant surprise, however. While I was waiting for the cabin door to open and we were allowed on the air bridge, almost below me a hatch was opened, and a few men started transferring suitcases to carts. To my extreme relief I recognized mine, so far so good! It was a pity the window didn't open so I could have asked them to take good care of it.

Arrival and departure were both via the Lindbergh terminal, so no transfers were needed. And yes, I did know who Lindbergh was. According to a map shops and eateries were mainly concentrated in The Mall, which I found without any difficulties. Many of the shops were closed, but they didn't interest me in the least anyhow. In a quiet branch I found a small restaurant offering snacks and espresso, so I snacked and espressoed. The espresso was very tiny and very expensive, but very good. In fact I felt like eating more, my biological clock was slightly out of whack. During my trip through part of North America I would pass through three of their four time zones: in Detroit the difference was six hours with the Netherlands, here in Minneapolis (and I presume in St Paul as well) seven, and later in Rapid City it would be eight hours.

To appease my rebellious stomach I went to an Arby's stand offering sliced beast sandwiches, according to the signs it was even supposed to be dead cow.

A blonde with a grin that could not be any wider without ripping her ears greeted me with a ridiculously large overdose of enthusiasm. I assured her that I wanted to look at the menu a bit more, turned back to her again after thirty seconds, and got a replay of the same overdone exuberance tape.

Now I know perfectly well that not all blondes are dumb, but on my account this one could develop a bit more initiative than unthinkingly following a script. I felt like removing her batteries if she showed the tendency to start again.

Armed with a sandwich, a soft drink and a helping of fries from the stand next-door because the blond grin didn't sell those, I found a table with a view of the busy airport apron activities. The sun was friendly enough to set with spectacular colors, which only improved the view.

Otherwise there was very little to do, as I said most stores had closed already, the restaurants offered little else interesting to occupy me. So I looked up the gate where I would wait for my next flight.

For the last leg of my trip I got a seat on an Airbus 319, with space for only about 125 passengers. I was glad there wouldn't be a next leg, it probably would have been in an old biplane with an open cockpit.

During the taxiing to the end of the airstrip we passed the Minnesota Air National Guard hangars. That all or at least some states had their own bit of air force kind of amazed me. In my mind's eye, and what a nice expression that is, I saw luridly painted biplanes from two Dutch provinces in a fierce dogfight, while the blimp from a neighboring third kept an eye on them.

The flight in the dark was rather interesting; towns and villages dotted the landscape as brightly illuminated stars. Even Seattle's dirty water couldn't ruin that, nor the fact that this plane was looking much more decrepit than the previous two.

* * *

Yet another color of carpet registered with me as we as I entered the Rapid City terminal building at almost ten that night. Automatically I checked the signs, then I walked with the rest of the freshly landed herd along shops and restaurants, all closed because of the late hour. Rapid City had a clearly smaller airport than the ones I dragged myself through during my last two stops, and so within a reasonable time I arrived downstairs at the merry-go-round where those who had walked faster had been waiting for their luggage already. After about ten minutes my trusty old suitcase dropped from a hatch decorated with rubber on the belt, and I could head to the exit.

An aged gentleman manned, in his case gentlemanned, a stand that supplied all sorts of Information totally free of charge. Since I had not reserved a rental car till the next day, after a night of catching my breath, I asked him what would be the best way to get to my hotel. He directed me to a desk a bit further along, where I could report for a free shuttle bus. Great service! Odd country, as said before, often screamingly expensive, then totally free.

I requested my free ride, and parked myself on a bench for what turned out to be a short wait before the driver entered and asked us to follow him. A few fellow travelers were waiting there already. The sliding doors slid open, and I grasped for air. In spite of it being dark already the heat struck me almost physically in my face.

The bus was parked neatly at the curb, and the driver helped us getting our luggage on board. As soon as we were seated we were carried through the darkness towards town. I got impressions of hills and mainly commercial buildings, otherwise nothing worth mentioning, but my tiredness also may have had something to do with that. A few stops at other hotels, then it was my turn. The driver brought my suitcase in, possibly more to get his voucher for the ride than to be of service to me.

The lobby, with much rustic wood and lounges on both sides, was furnished in a clearly Wild West inspired way, complete with a wall filling hearth, but with a now dark television set instead of a fireplace.

The receptionist welcomed me with a smile that a sympathetic person as myself naturally triggers. The fact that I was a paying customer was totally irrelevant, naturally.

Really.

“Welcome! Do you have a reservation?”

“Certainly. The name is Versluys, with u y.”

She looked puzzled.

“With me why what?”

Some things work better in another language, I guess. I decided to show her my passport, and she got it.

The first impression is always the best, and I screwed up yet another one.

Through a corridor, into an elevator, after a suitable pause out of the elevator, another corridor, a side corridor, and a surprisingly large and well-furnished room with a private bathroom that Ria would have taken home at the drop of a hat. Good thing she wasn't here, I didn't need any more penalty points with the receptionist.

The breakfast buffet the next morning was well enough supplied for an orphanage and a half. Besides regular fare like bread, yoghurt and eggs there were cupcakes, bagels, donuts, some unclear kind of buns over which my fellow eaters spread an unknown to me gooey stuff, several kinds of cornflakes and even a contraption that dispensed batter for the waffle iron next to it. There was an enormous double coffee urn, accompanied by a machine that promised to add extra flavors. The coffee, without scary flavors, naturally, was reasonable – not Dutch, but certainly not Seattle either.

There were a few racks with brochures of attractions and sights far and near, of which I selected immodestly, as a journalist - which I was supposed to be, remember? - one never has enough background materials. At the reception there were some maps of the city and the area, which I addled to my new collection.

After enjoying the almost indecently expansive breakfast the bus transported me back to the airport. The Alamo people obviously did know a set of wheels had been reserved for me. The friendly lady – what an enormous number of those there were in what they quite justifiably call the "service industry" – also would like to know what my plans were, but for unclear reasons had to grin when I told her I'd be staying in Porcupine.

She remarked that I probably came from a big city, since I was the third Dutchman from that place within a month. That surprised me to no end, Benedenveensloot-

Tweededwarsdiep isn't all that big – basically two rows of houses, one on either side of a defunct canal. The surprise disappeared when the lady asked how I pronounced the name of my city, but pointed at the word "Rijbewijs" – Dutch for driving license. My correction was delivered with a maximal helping of tact.

After the exchange of documents and credit card data, me promising to return the car with a full tank, and swearing a holy oath that I'd never ever even consider smoking in the car I was told where I could find a shiny Hyundai. She was correct, it was right there.

Calmly I wheeled myself back to town, where almost immediately I was nearly ran off the road by somebody who obviously won her driver's license only two days before at the local bingo, and now enthusiastically crossed from a driveway at my right to the left hand lane, right in front of my bumper.

Armed with information and recent experiences I first visited one of those horrible huge megastores, one of which I knew to be located near my hotel. An extension cord was on my list – I did have an adaptor plug so my Dutch plugs with their fat round prongs could be used with a US wall socket – but I had noticed in the past that some extra latitude never is a bad thing. Naturally a headset for the return flight went into the oversized shopping cart, and remembering Ria I added a second one.

At the other side of the store, perhaps half a mile away, I remembered one of the Postmas' tips and loaded 24 bottles of drinking water, collected in a plastic shroud, on my cart. I took a quick look at food for the trip, but sandwiches with blue speckled bologna didn't quite appeal to me, so I decided to try my luck on the road. To misquote the famous Gallic sage Asterix: “Those Americans are crazy.”

A bit further down the same street I found another store I needed: a print shop. I handed them my thumb drive and a few minutes later I received 100 prints of the mini-poster I had hobbied together before I left. It showed pictures of Eddy and Natasja, and asked for information on how I could contact them. The phone numbers were mine and of the trading post – naturally I had to remember to tell them they had voluntarily agreed to add theirs.

In the meantime I had found out that the local accent differed a lot from the singing sounds of the “Southern drawl” that I had encountered in Georgia. That was more pleasant to listen to, but also harder to understand than the sharper tones that were flooding my ears over here. A second point was a confirmation of my Georgian experiences: the average American is friendly and helpful.

According to Mr. Google there were two roads from Rapid City to the reservation: a shorter one through the Badlands, and a somewhat longer one bypassing the reservation by a more westerly route, which would let me enter Pine Ridge from the south. I decided to take the latter because I wanted to get an impression of the Black Hills.

Before I left I toyed with the radio a bit, and to my joy I managed to extract a country & western station from the ether, with Willie Nelson presenting non-stop golden oldies.

I crossed through the town center, navigating by one of the maps I found at the hotel reception, and without too much of an effort found Mount Rushmore Road.
Luckily I also found a location of a well-known and way overpriced string of coffee shops, but at least one I could trust also to make real coffee besides their fashion drinks. Three espressos later I continued my way south, out of town, into the Black Hills.

* * *

To be honest, and you should know by now I'm always honest with you, I wasn't really overly impressed by the Black Hills right away. To me it appeared to be an Americanized version of not really high mountainous area like the Eiffel or the Sauerland at our Eastern neighbors. Naturally there were differences: the billboards, the un-German relaxed traffic with a high pick-up truck content, for instance. Even though the season was supposed to be over already there were still plenty of campers on their way, from built-up pick-ups to behemoths the size of a Greyhound bus.
According to the billboards there must have been an attraction every few hundred yards that I just had to visit, so I passed them.
I followed a well maintained two lane highway further into the hills. Slowly the billboards diminished, and the character of the smooth rolling hills changed, rough irregular granite boulders and peaks appeared, and the hills seemed to be higher, and somewhere I even passed through a tunnel dug through a rock that happened to be crossing the road.

I passed the national park entrance, and indeed, the occasional park ranger jeep was added to the traffic mix. Still at a sedate pace the traffic meandered along, into the ever rougher landscape. Narrow hollows alternated with wider ones, coniferous forests with meadows.

And then all of a sudden there it was. I came around yet another curve, and saw slightly to the side in front of me, across a wide dale, one of the best known places in the United States: Mount Rushmore, the four gigantic president's heads hewn from the granite rock face. A handy and undoubtedly not accidentally installed parking lot was in use by two cars, but there was ample space so I joined them.

Because of the distance it took a while till it dawned on me how large those heads actually were, but the fully grown trees in front of them provided me with a good reference.

Every once in a while a car stopped, the occupants got out and took pictures, usually including one of them. I also took some pictures though without me in them, then sat for a while on the crash barrier with a bottle of water.

It may sound funny, but sitting there on that crash barrier for the first time I really had the feeling that I actually was in America, probably because I now took the time to let everything soak in as opposed to just registering things on the run.

It was a pity that I now also had time to think of Eddy and Natasja again. I was hoping to be only a few hours away from them by now, but would I be able to locate them in this literally alien land? What sort of local contacts or reinforcements had Pater manage to organize for me, if any at all?

With a sigh I got up from my improvised seat. The empty water bottle disappeared in a trash can installed especially for that purpose by the National Park Service. With a fresh bottle I crawled back behind the wheel.

A little further down I passed the main entrance of the park surrounding Mount Rushmore, but as I said, I passed it.

To my surprise I saw Mount Rushmore again a few miles later: suddenly I saw George Washington in between two peaks. Here again there was a tactically located parking lot, that I used gratefully to get a last impression of this very special place.

The road weaved on through the hills, and I weaved neatly along in the row of vehicles.

As promised the Crazy Horse monument was not far away. I took a left and drove immediately into a trap formed by cash registers. I paid a seemingly high entrance fee, for which I was allowed to take along an additional three passengers. I didn't have any of those, but it's the gesture that counts, as those who only gesture always say. The dearly paid for road led to a spacious parking lot with besides a many headed herd of cars and campers a respectable row of busses. Tourist season might officially be over, here too plenty was still going on.

At first glance the main building mainly resembled a classical mountain hotel, at second glance it still did, I tried, really. At the entrance my ticket was checked, and I came into a spacious hall with on one side information booths, and hallways leading in various directions.

If I had to describe the building, and as a writer I do see that as a moral obligation to the readers, both of them, then 'museum' would be the most fitting term. Display cases were filled with old and not very old Indian handicraft. There was a complete teepee, a canoe and a sweat lodge, and a scale model of the mountain with the artwork finished, way too much to really take it in during the short time I had allowed myself here.

From the wooden panorama deck I had a great view of the mountain and the enormous statue under construction. A bus ambling up the road to it helped realize how gigantic this sculpture was, the already monumental Mount Rushmore sculptures were dwarfed by it.

My suspicious mind actually harbored the idea that nobody was in a rush to finish the colossus, because it was now attracting more visitors than it would once finished.

I went down the mountain and took a left, in the direction of Pine Ridge, though that was not posted on any signs yet.

Now I passed along fire scorched hills, I had heard something about huge fires in the United States but that was before I heard I was going here, so I never really placed it. Enormous areas now only existed of gray-black hills, or if it had been a forest, it now was a spooky collection of thousands of enormous blackened tooth picks.

Every here and there farms were alternated with antiques shops, each and every one of them closed as if they figured already I wasn't going to spend any money there anyhow.

What puzzled me for a while were the old car tires that hung every here and there from the barbed wire of the fields alongside the road. When I had a bit of a better look I noticed many had writing on them in white paint, and it dawned on me that these were the local version of "private – no trespassing" signs.

A deer that was looking at me from the side of the road didn't contradict me, so it had to be true.

The road took me through a number of towns. Some looked like escapees from a Wild West movie while others had a more Victorian feeling. In Custer a retired caboose and a repurposed old railway station reminded of the train that once rode there, and a bit further down Hot Springs had a stream and even a waterfall near the town center. I could imagine the town just about crawling with tourists during the summer, and I didn't miss them at all.

I noticed a well-known fast food name next to the road and decided to enjoy a hamburger, a helping of fries and an utterly delicious caramel milkshake. It started with the usual oversized bucket. In it came caramel syrup, followed by the usual ice-cream and milk mixture. That got the blender treatment. A high domed lid topped the bucket, and it was filled to the top with whipped cream. A bit more caramel syrup completed the construction. So, the US does have its good sides, as long as you ignore the diabetes risk. Just a pity they're having such a hard time making a decent cup of coffee…

Pleasantly full I hit the road again. In the meantime I figured out how the road verges were kept so immaculately clean. Not only here but also there discrete roadside signs informed the interested passer-by which section of verge had been adopted by what organization, and was maintained by them. Another odd American conception that actually worked.

Just outside Hot Springs I got on highway 385, and for the first time I could push the gas pedal down a bit more. The hills had made space for a rolling landscape, once prairie, now mainly parched fields and meadows.

Just before reaching the town of Oelrichs I turned left, on highway 18. The Hyundai and me hopped across an unguarded railway crossing and blasted east again, at first along a ruler straight road, but eventually though a varying hilly landscape. Every here and there I noticed a small hill that looked like it had to be put there by a gigantic dump truck, but which were natural after all.

Here also I saw scorched fields in between the dry ones, enormous areas must have been burned. The map had informed me that I was now driving east parallel to the Nebraska border, but that knowledge didn't cause any notable emotions, so I won't tell you of those then.

A sign assured me that the building complex at the right of the road was the Prairie Winds Casino, a modest source of income for several area reservations. It also meant I was getting close to my destination.

A little further along the road was the village of Oglala, as far as I could tell from the road hardly more than a uniform collection of trailer homes and a small church.

From a distance I saw one of those typical American water towers, an upside-down onion on a tall leg, announcing that I was arriving in Pine Ridge.

Pine Ridge had exactly one traffic light, and it was red. To my right I saw what I assumed to be government offices, and across from them a large gas station. To the left in front of me I spotted a few small restaurants with larger buildings behind them. Some people ambled along the sidewalks, going any faster was not recommended in this heat.

The light changed to green, and I followed highway 18 to the left. More shops, a strange round building that I couldn't identify, a far from glamorous gas station and dilapidated wooden houses caught my attention.

Outside of town there were some storage buildings between the road and the airfield, some appeared to be in disrepair. At the other side were some abandoned and obviously derelict wooden houses.

After a field filled with dead sunflowers I turned left, on Big Foot Trail.

The postal address for the trading post where I would be staying was Porcupine, so I followed the road past Wounded Knee cemetery and museum. The reasonably flat road had meadows at both sides.

The hills determining the left and right side horizons had some oddly craggy peaks which somehow reminded me a bit of medieval castle towers. At irregular intervals an unpaved side road lead to a group of trailers or a simple house. The unavoidable written-off car tires were dangling here as well at undoubtedly carefully selected spots from poles that kept up barbed wire. Beautiful horses, quarterhorses I would learn later, shared a total lack of interest in me with great looking palominos and black cows.

Porcupine was mainly situated to the side of the main road, and at first fleeting glance appeared to consist of a randomly planted collection of single story buildings.

What I didn't spot was a sign indicating I had arrived at the trading post, and according to Google I should have passed it several kilometers/miles/minutes ago.

So I turned the car around and went back. Still no sign, and no houses to ask for directions near the road.

Suddenly I noticed a long low building on my right, according to a sign seniors housing. Some people were standing outside taking, and I had their full attention when I entered the parking lot. I got out, stretched, and wandered to a man who, till my arrival, had been chatting with a lady who was leaning out of a window.

I told them that I was looking for the trading post, and they knew right away what I meant. Good sign, obviously it wasn't too far away anymore. After a short discussion the man drew a map on the reverse of my printed route description. They explained that I should have turned left at the Wounded Knee memorial after all, but now it was smarter to continue till I got to a major side road, Gooseneck Road. Totally for free they added the tip that if I saw the Sharps Corner store, I had gone too far.

Gooseneck Road I found leading across the hills separating the wrong from the right valley, and it must have been closely related to a rollercoaster. Signs with lazily reclining arrows urgently reminded you at curves to follow those. Since I'm a decent guy and still had a good name to protect over here I followed the advice. Here in the hills there were also burnt patches, but smaller than the ones I saw elsewhere.

At the end of the road I turned right, and almost immediately I spotted the trading post's sign. I couldn't see a building yet, but the gate on a dirt road was invitingly open. I accepted the invitation and produced an impressive dust cloud as I followed the road up a low rise.

The trading post was a largish two story building in log cabin style. The bottom front was wrapped in a porch, wooden outside stairs led up to the second floor door. In front of the building was some playground equipment, across from it a few shed-like structures. In a meadow were some, in my untrained eye, nice looking horses.

As soon as I got out of the car I was greeted by three friendly dogs of undetermined breed. They accompanied me to the store.

I greeted the three ladies who were present: a blonde and two Native American ones, and introduced myself.

The blonde lady turned out to be Susie, the owner. She assured me my room had been readied, and she was pleased that the Postmas sent their regards.

She showed the way up the outside stairs, through a screen door, into the bed and breakfast's living room. Adjoining the sitting area was a long dining table, to the left a modern kitchen, to the right two guest rooms with a bathroom in between them. The first room turned out to be mine.

No air conditioning, but luckily the large refrigerator in the kitchen sported an ice cube and cold water dispenser. I asked if I needed a key in case I went out at night, but Susie assured me the door was never locked. If I really insisted I could get dinner besides my breakfast, but she didn't sound overly eager. I assured her I would warn her in a timely fashion should the need arise.

After a short hesitation I told her why I really was there. She thought for a moment, but said she had heard nothing about either Eddy or Natasja. She assured me she'd ask her staff. One of the ladies, Andrea, was living in Kyle, perhaps she could find out something. I doubted that, but

I wasn't in a position to refuse any help. She was fine with me adding her phone number to my posters, and kept one copy.

Susie disappeared via a narrow and steep inside staircase to the store downstairs, and I decided to freshen up a bit and go to bed early: I had some hunting to do tomorrow.

Innocent as always I switched on the bathroom light. At once there was rattling sound on the roof, as if somebody was banging two sheets of metal together. Carefully I looked up, but nothing fell on my head, so perhaps it was meant to be like that, and it was only the ventilation system. Perhaps just as well the nearest neighbors were over half a mile away!

A few hours later I was woken up by the dogs under my window howling along with others further away, or would those be coyotes?

Odd country, as I have concluded earlier.

III

Kyle College was hard to overlook. The town itself was probably a bit further, still out of view. First I saw to the left the Lakota Prairie Ranch Resort where Eddy and Natasja were supposed to be. Completely in accordance with my expectations it was another single story building, quite long and with some campers behind it. The college was just about across from it, to the right of the road. It was an enormous round building with a forest of antennas on the roof. The parking was surrounded by a collection of offices etcetera. The Hyundai didn't mind staying behind on the hot asphalt all by itself to catch its breath after the ride while I entered the main building. In the meantime I noticed something going on a few hundred yards further down, people were walking up and down a hill topped with a large circular shelter-like structure. Drumming and singing could be heard in the distance, and an abundance of flags tried heroically but in vain to wave in the near absence of wind. Now I passed a row of tables where people were proudly displaying various kinds of vegetables and fruits.

Inside I understood even less. The information desk was unmanned, and the first rooms I entered were occupied by people showing beautifully made beadwork. It may have been a competition, but I could be wrong. Incredible as it may seem, my knowledge of the international beadwork competition circuit is virtually non-existent. Please accept my insincere apologies for this lack of essential information, pictures of me in sackcloth and ashes may be obtained from the publisher if so desired.

A bit bedazzled by this unexpected cultural immersion I went out again, only to run almost immediately into the arms of a petite lady with a clipboard. It is a well-established fact that you can ask people with clipboards anything at any moment, so I asked her where I might find doctor Two Horses.

Clipboard Lady smiled.

“Mike? He’s dancing.”

My total lack of understanding must have been abundantly clear. She pointed to the hill.

“We’re having a wacipi this weekend, Mike always is one of the dancers. You can recognize him by his red regalia.”

Okay, I clearly wasn’t at home anymore…

I followed the concrete footpath to the shelter. I wasn’t alone, groups of people were coming and going. Half way down I was ambushed by three children selling me an overpriced bottle of water, the proceeds were intended for a school project. In the desiccated field next to the path boys were participating in unknown, to me at least, sports. Once again my general knowledge, of which I am usually so justifiably proud, was found to be seriously lacking. Nothing works as well for subduing an overactive ego as a sudden immersion into a different culture, especially one that obviously differed quite a bit from the way Hollywood had taught me.

The shelter I found to be much larger than I first thought, it was a large circular structure around a dry grassy field, with low tiers of seats in its shade. Behind it were rows of cars and pick-up trucks, and every here and there a sales stand.

The drumming and singing originated from a group of men seated around a huge drum between two sections of tiers, with all of them drumming to accompany their singing. A boy dangled a microphone over the drum.

The large round arena was in use by several dozen dancers, from little girls to venerable elderly ladies. All were gaily and beautifully fitted out. Some held wonderful shawls spread out like the wings of a bird, others wore dresses with dozens, perhaps hundreds, of shiny tubular bells which accompanied their every move with their jingling. It was a great spectacle, with each participant celebrating their own dancing feast.

A moment's break was followed by another short bit of music, then the singing died down. The loudspeakers informed me that I had witnessed an "intertribal", and after a break of a minute or so some men entered the arena. They appeared to be the jury, and the announcers called out the names of the winners in the various age categories. Happy adults gratefully accepted their prizes, exalted little girls ran smiling to their families in the audience, a few dollar bills in their hands.

Now the announcers asked the men to enter, and specifically the adults. One after another they appeared from the shelter's shade into the fiery sunshine. In the meantime I was having a problem, I had totally exhausted my supply of superlatives on the ladies and now I was totally without. And it was so spectacular! All the colors of the rainbow, headdresses and back decorations (bustles, I learned later) with hundreds of eagle feathers, beadwork, mirrors, fir cuffs around the ankles, beautifully beaded moccasins, it was an avalanche of impressions. Some were carrying stylized weapons.

A new drum sounded, and the surrounding group of singers joined in. The dancers began a dance that took them clockwise around. Each seemed to have their own style, some shuffled sedately, others jumped about with unbridled enthusiasm. From the audience yells of encouragement sounded. An elderly man didn't seem too impressed by it all but danced his rounds with simple steps, totally immersed in what he was doing, while his younger colleagues were whirling past him.

I realized the near total absence of non-natives and concluded this was the real thing, just the Lakota amongst themselves, not something put up for the tourists.

Somewhere my non-Euro penny dropped and I understood something of the cultural clash between the white newcomers and the original inhabitants of these lands. How much of what had gone dreadfully wrong in the past would have started out as a plain misunderstanding based on a lack of knowledge of each other? I'm just saying, if you ran into people like these totally unprepared or armed with our modern knowledge, you'd have to swallow once or twice, wouldn't you, especially considering coming from a time and culture where everybody not known personally was automatically classified as at least suspect, more likely as an enemy.

In the meantime I still hadn't the faintest idea who Mike Two Horses was. Red regalia, the clipboadesse had said (she was well past the age of being called a clipboardette, one has to be precise in these matters) but I had no idea what part of the outfits qualified as regalia. I didn't have a clue, and red was a common color, appearing in nearly all the costumes.

Again that short break, followed by a short encore of drumming and singing, and it was over. Sweating and sometimes panting the men were waiting for the jury. Loud applause accompanied the announcement of the winners and the handing out of the envelopes with the prize money.

Proudly the dancers returned to their families to be received with compliments and bottles of water.

I decided to make my rounds to track down Two Horses. Almost immediately I ran into the elderly dancer, behind my section of tiered seats. He look both exhausted and exalted. I introduced myself and asked if he knew Two Horses.

"Mike is my nephew, I'm his uncle."

"Do you know where he is now?"

He gestured vaguely to the other side.

"Just look out for a white van, he should be there now."

I strolled around the stands, and passed behind the jury and announcer's platform. Now I noticed there were more drum groups than the two I heard so far, spread out around the arena, some were silently rehearsing their next number. Everywhere families were picnicking.

What I also noticed is that there were a lot of vans, and that more than half of them were white. I decided to ask again. The first man I asked showed clearly by his behavior that he didn't consider me to be one of the invitees, the second pointed out the right van. A sturdily built man, who I recognized indeed as one of the dancers, was sitting in the shade, talking lively with two young boys.

Again I introduced myself, and yes, this time it was the right man. The regalia appeared to be his complete outfit, though his shirt on the other hand was green. He had taken off his headdress and bustle already.

"You are a friend of Eddy's?"

"We've known each other quite a few years already, and went through some stuff together. When I heard that Natasja and he had disappeared I decided to come."

Mike sighed.

"I sincerely hope you'll succeed in finding them, but I have no idea what I could tell you that could help. We don't know what happened, and at the hotel they don't know anything either. One moment they were there, the next they were gone."

"And he never talked about what was going on?"

"Not a word. Our last conversation was about our work, nothing exiting I fear."

He pointed at an unoccupied folding chair. One after another I took the seat and a sip from my bottle.

"I know nothing and nobody over here. Any suggestions how I can handle my investigations best?"

I pulled a copy of my "wanted" poster from my chest pocket, and presented it to him. He scanned it quickly, and nodded.

"That is a start. Make your rounds, make a chat everywhere people come together, and ask if you can put up one of these. One tip, and please don't take this the wrong way. You'll have to talk differently."

I didn't get it.

"You talk like a white man, a dialogue. Like we're having now. And Indian expects that he can tell his whole story, and take his time for it, and that you will wait till he's finished. By all means tell your story, then wait quietly for him to tell you what he wants to tell you, even if it takes a while."

"Doesn't sound all that different, to be honest."

"It is, believe me. Just try it out during your expedition."

He got up, and got a bag from the car. He took a calling card out of it.

"Call me when you need me or if you learn anything, day or night. That's your number on the poster, I assume?"

My head made a nodding movement, and I explained that the other number belonged to the trading post.

"Then I can promise the same, I'll call you the minute I hear something."

We shook hands, and I took my leave while he put his headdress back on, and fasted it with a string under his chin.

* * *

The village of Manderson was comprised out of a number of seemingly identical houses, glued against a slope to the side of the road, overlooking fewer houses on flatter terrain at the other side. The center was a dusty open space on both sides of the road. There was no traffic at all, so the road was hardly more than a friendly suggestion right now.

On one side, in the shade of a bunch of sad looking trees, stood a bunker-like construction that, judging by the poor state of maintenance, had been through a handful of wars and which was, according to a sign, harboring the one and only original post office. Look, they had next to nothing down there, but they did have a post office, something long extinct in the Netherlands. Sometimes I really don't understand things, and I really do try. Obviously practice doesn't make perfect all of the time.

On the other side was a pastel colored single story building named Pinky's, surrounded by some cars and a modest herd of pick-up trucks. It somewhat resembled the convenience store at Sharps Corner I visited on my way back from Kyle yesterday, only this one lacked gas pumps.

I planted my shiny silvery grey riding can in between two ageing and no longer shining pick-up trucks, and went in.

Various heads went up and watched me suspiciously unsuspicious. I greeted the girl at the cash register, and pulled a bottle of soda from one of the coolers at the wall to my left. The shelves were home to more stuff that could pass as food than those at their colleagues at that Sharps Corner, but the prices were just as high over here. After some searching I found a package of what I recognized as pastry. A machine on a counter assured me that it would put molten cheese on tortilla chips, at a reasonable price, but my travel insurance probably didn't cover self-inflicted harm, and anyhow I figured myself too young for such a horrible fate.

The young lady at the checkout accepted my cash, while two local gentlemen studied hand written lists with what seemed to be high school sports competitions bets. With my carbonated beverage and my pastry I wandered to the long and currently unoccupied table in the store. I sat down with my back to some freezers and a door that led, according to a sign, to a laundromat, so I had a good view of nearly all of the shop.

The other customers kept circulating, but everybody happened to have to pass close to me. Or two times. Or three. I got the impression that visitors from elsewhere were a rare occurrence here. That was probably due to the before mentioned lack of traffic on the road through town.

As I was half way through my soda an about thirty years old slim and tall man dressed in an extremely clean shirt dumped a cardboard box on the table two seats away from me on. With a box cutter he started dissecting the box with movements bred by years of experience. I pile of unknown to me packages began taking shape between us. He took one of those price label tools, and while he was setting it, he just happened to look my way, and he nodded.

"Hi, how are you doing?"

I answered his greeting with a similar empty commonplace remark.

"Tourist?"

I shook my head, and took another sip, while he waited patiently.

"Actually I'm looking for a friend of mine."

He waited, but I didn't add anything.

"Somebody from around here?"

Again I shook my head, and I got a poster out of my bag.

"Also from the Netherlands, just like me. Kamminga, Eddy Kamminga is his name. He's supposed to be around here, together with his Natasja."

I was really paying close attention but couldn't spot any reaction as he studied the photographs. Now it was his turn to shake his head. With a shrug he returned the piece of paper.

"Never heard of them, never seen them either. Is he a tourist?"

"No, a scientist."

And eyebrow was raised by way of question mark.

"A scientist? What kind? Historian?"

"As far as I know he came here to investigate the drinking water. That's the kind of stuff he does, at a university."

The man looked at me.

"A waste of time. We are perfectly well aware that our water is polluted by naturally appearing uranium, and chemicals from the former military practice ranges up there in the Badlands. We're also aware it is damaging our elders' kidneys, and that dialysis is doing not enough, and usually comes too late. I'm wondering why he really was here."

I looked him in the eye.

"I think you're making a valid point, but he has already come up with some clever ways to remove junk from water, perhaps he wanted to give it a try over here."

It sounded right in my ears, but obviously not in shop dude's.

“And what company wants to earn money at our expense now?”

Obviously I had stepped on some very sensitive long toes.

“No company, he came here to work with Two Horses of the Kyle College.”

That cleared the air more than a little.

“Ah, the college, that’s something else then. And your friend is over there?”

“Was over there, he and his wife disappeared from their hotel.”

Now I really had his attention.

“And nobody at the college knows anything either?”

I shook my head in the internationally accepted manner.

He thought for a moment.

“We don’t get to hear much over here, but should I hear something…”

I returned one of my mini posters to him, with the complete names and descriptions of Eddy and Natasja, as well as the number to which my cell phone reacted, should I remember to feed the battery in time.

“And where are you going now?”

Still in my international mode I shrugged with both my shoulders. My perfectly developed sense of international non-verbal communication sure came in handy.

“Have you been to Wounded Knee yet?”

“No, only passed it yesterday. I’m only just beginning.”

“Those guys over there get to see a lot of tourists, perhaps they have seen or heard something.

I thanked him, and went back to my tin can.

The village of Wounded Knee was on the same road, and was hard to miss. Immediately past the village I could see on a hill to my left the chapel belonging to the monument. Beyond that I came to a T-junction with the Pine Ridge to Porcupine road. Across the way I saw a parking strip, a sign and some stands, only one of which seemed to be occupied.

I parked my car on the therefore automatically not anymore deserted parking strip, and strolled over to the sign describing the 1890 massacre of hundreds of unarmed Sioux. Remarkable was that the word "massacre" was written on a separate piece of board which was applied over the original text.

"Originally it said "battle"," a voice next to me sounded, "till too many protests came, so they changed it into the truth."

A man of about twenty-five, wearing rather worn jeans, had joined me, a few necklaces in his hand. The man told me the massacre story, and pointed out the cemetery on the hillock across the road, the actual monument proper.

Again I made one of my posters appear from thin air – or my shoulder bag, I forget which. He perused it attentively, but in the end had to shake his head.

"I'm sorry, I don't remember seeing them."

He pointed at the stand, crewed by a young couple.

"Perhaps they know something, they're here every day."

Before I could go over to his colleagues he showed me a nice looking colorful beaded necklace which he was willing to let me have for an, according to him, friendly price.

The next conversation supplied just as little by way of information, but I did buy a dream catcher, but they wanted to hold on to my poster and promised to call me if they heard anything.

The impression popped up in my head that I might have to interview all of the forty thousand people on the reservation separately…

Under the watchful eye of the three souvenir sellers as well as the burning sun I ambled up the hill, to the cemetery gate. It looked deserted up there, but that was deceptive. As soon as I passed through the gate I was encountered by two young men, waiting on either side in the shade.

"Welcome to Wounded Knee!"

They told me the story of this cemetery which was a combination of monument to the 1890 victims and the current Wounded Knee village cemetery. Within a chain-link enclosure was a long rectangular barren space with only some barren weeds and the odd dried up sprig of grass. A concrete path surrounded a wide strip along the center. To the right was a huge granite marker. Outside the chain-link enclosure were the later graves.

"That is the mass grave. You may enter, but please walk only on the concrete path."

I opened the gate and slowly walked my round. It was a strange place, to be honest very barren and simple, and perhaps that's what made it so impressive. Some desiccated twigs of sage I noticed on the mass grave, as a homage to the victims. Everywhere colorful ribbons were tied to the fence, I assumed as a kind of prayer. As I got closer I noticed a long list of names chiseled on all four sides of the marker.

At the foot of the monument were simple offerings; flowers, stones, a bottle of water, a flag, you name it. I had not counted on this, this was an obvious oversight in my hurried preparations. I dug in my pockets, but found nothing suitable. There were a few coins there already, and not quite contented I added a Dutch two Euro piece.

Not totally unexpected the duo at the gate ambushed me as I attempted to leave, to sell me some necklaces. After shedding a few bit of green paper with portraits of dead presidents on them I showed the poster. Both studied the pictures attentively, but here also no bulbs lit up. They did want to keep the poster, however.

As I trudged down the hill I thought about how friendly, helpful and polite the young people I met here were. Okay, they wanted to relieve me of a few bucks, but didn't do so in an overly pushy way.

Slightly discouraged I drove on to Pine Ridge. Now that I had gotten started I began to realize how expansive and unknown the area was, and that I really didn't have a clue if I was doing something sensible. But what else could I do? Doing nothing naturally was not an option, I could only hope that I would unintentionally do something right.

* * *

A handful of posters and fruitless talks later I figured I deserved something to eat. I had noticed a Mexican place on the main road, and decided to honor it with a visit. The place wasn't overly large, but business looked brisk, at least half of the ten or so tables were occupied.

The friendly chubby young lady behind the counter didn't know Eddy or Natasja either, but was willing to supply me with food and drink. I chose some burritos, a churro and a soft drink, and sat at a table at the window.

Carefully I stuck one end of a burrito in my head, while holding my pint of soda at the ready, in case something went wrong. To prove that men are able to do more than one thing at the same time (the word "multitasking" has also been adopted by the Dutch language already) I kept an eye on the long package containing, according to aforementioned smiling chubby young lady behind the counter, a microwaved churro. Well, it didn't look like any I had encountered in civilization. At least it didn't move, I considered that a positive point, so the microwaves had done their job well and had given no quarter.

The table I had picked was outfitted for four people. Besides me and my shoulder bag, which was now catching its breath next to me, there was still space for two more victims, three if I'd remove the bag from its well-deserved spot. The number of unoccupied seats was reduced by one by a man of about twenty-five years old, dressed in a T-shirt advertising a Rapid City car repair shop that looked like it had been washed at least a hundred times, dusty slightly worn jeans with a belt with an enormous not totally undamaged buckle in the shape of a pick-up truck. I couldn't see his feet but assumed a pair of dusty and clearly worn boots down there. He planted a small bucket of soda in front of him on the table. The bucket had a neat plastic lid so not a drop was spilled during this operation

"Enjoy your meal!" he grinned, showing off a well maintained set of teeth.

I confirmed I was giving it my best shot, and wondered what he was trying to sell. I didn't see any dreamcatchers, but that didn't mean a thing; necklaces and bracelets take up much less space.

"I am Billie White Owl," he declared. It rang no bells.

"Wim," I replied.

"Wim Verslois, I know, please to make your acquaintance."

As you may have noticed by now my last name poses an insurmountable problem for most non-Dutch since I don't know of any other language with an "ui" or in my case "uy" sound. By the way, my family name means either "lockkeeper" or "person living at/near a lock." I have no idea which of my ancestors was responsible for that, but since last names became mandatory around 1810 when Napoleon was Emperor it must have been at that time or earlier.

The first bite of the burrito didn't hurt a bit and had been washed down by now, so I dared taking a second. In the meantime I had learned that if these people want to tell you something they will. He did. So Mike Two Horses had been right after all with his mini-lecture on Indian conversational techniques.

"I'd like to pass on the regards of a mutual friend."

I raised one of my eyebrows a few millimeters by way of encouragement to continue. Eddy?

"Pater is his name. He told me to tell you he's looking forward to your next boat outing"

I nodded.

"And you are from…?"

He nodded as well.

“If you don’t mind I’d just as soon not show you my credentials right here right now, but I’m a genuine colleague of Pater’s. Special agent.”

So, from the aforementioned FBI. Or maybe from another cluster of letters, I never quite understood their system.

I didn’t quite get the “special” bit either. If I order special fries back home I’ll get it with a combo of mayo, ketchup, chopped onions and perhaps some peanut sauce, but somehow I didn’t see that fitting in this case. Hopefully his partner (m/f) can appreciate the “special” bit also without the additional condiments. Oops, never mind that (m/f) bit, considering his employer.

“I could imagine you being a bit less obvious than me around here,” was the first thing that came to my mind.

He shook his head, grinning.

“Unless I say something. I happen to be a Sicangu.”

Okay, that must have been another chapter I hadn’t read yet. I might not even own the book at all.

“Is it contagious?”

He bared a lot of teeth.

“Sicangu, or Brule. That is a different Lakota band than the local Oglala. We speak the same language, Lakota, but they’ll probable be able to tell by my accent that I’m from the Rosebud reservation, a bit further East. They couldn’t find an Oglala at such a short notice.”

And thus you learn something new every day, whether you want to or not. In this manner I have turned into a virtual walking storage of usually totally useless bits of information. One day people will come to me for information instead of Wikipedia. Yeah, right.

“What has been undertaken so far to find Eddy and Natasja?”
He sighed.
“We’ve been asking around. We mapped the various possibilities, so we can conduct our search efforts more effectively.”
I looked at him.
“Never go into politics, your delivery is far from perfect. You guys don’t have the faintest idea, right?”
Renewed sigh.
“Almost completely correct, but a theory was suggested that I’d like to bounce off you now.”
“Bounce away.”
He hesitated a moment.
“I know Kamminga is your friend, but he has initiated contact with criminals before.”
See, ‘Waddengoud’ doesn’t have to be translated, he knew the contents already. Eddy made a huge error in judgement, but eventually ended up with Natasja, and all of us with a comfortable amount of cash.
“I presume you have a good reason for bringing this up?”
“Two reasons, even. This is a poor area, people are desperate. In spite of this being a dry area there’s a lot of alcohol in circulation, and plenty of drugs. I am under the impression Kamminga can manufacture both with ease, and it might be that he received an offer he couldn’t refuse. Drugs would be my first choice.”
Okay, Eddy did produce more than a little alcohol for use amongst friends, that much is true, and he’s darn good at that, but never for commercial purposes as far as I knew, and I figured I knew pretty far. And drugs?

Never ever! That was an abhorrence we've always shared.

"You also may know that Eddy is not exactly desperate for cash? Totally apart from the fact that he'd never manufacture anything like drugs."

"I may not have expressed myself totally clear. What I meant when I said they made him an offer he couldn't refuse I was thinking it might be why his wife disappeared as well."

For a moment I imagined a dungeon, with Natasja chained to a wall, and Eddy busy with beakers and stuff like that. I didn't like that image, but couldn't find a different one.

"Are there any organizations around here that could or would do something like that?"

"I don't know. I suspect so, but there's no hard evidence yet. It could be others, from outside, who appreciate the peace and quiet down here."

"Why did you say drugs were more likely? Wouldn't alcohol be a bigger market?"

"White Clay."

"Beg pardon?"

"Have a look yourself. Go back to the intersection at the gas station, the one with the traffic lights. Turn left. You're almost at the Nebraska border there, just a few minutes. Just across the border is White Clay. There are about ten people living there, between them they're running six or eight liquor stores. They thrive on the local ban on alcohol. Officially there's a fifty mile buffer zone around the reservation, but some way or another in 1904 an exception was made for White Clay. In other words, there is an abundance of alcohol. The tribal government is trying hard to change things, there's even talk of brewing their own beer, but it's all far from solved. Drugs are plentiful too, especially meth, but still not as abundant and obvious as alcohol."

That all sounded great, but that didn't help ridding Natasja of her chains, and I didn't want her to catch a cold in that chilly dungeon.

"So, what have you been up to?"

I told him of my fruitless conversations in Manderson, at Wounded Knee, and at the college. He nodded.

"I was afraid of that, we weren't getting any signals from those areas either. We'll just have to plod along."

I wasn't overjoyed by this lack of purposeful action by either of us, I'd have to come up with a way to do more.

"Not many other options, are there?"

"Oh, another thing. Word is you have been busy with your poster. Good plan. Have you been to the newspaper yet?"

"Where would that be, Rapid City?"

"No, the Lakota Country Times, in Martin."

My hazy look must have spoken for itself.

"The newspaper is for both the Pine Ridge and Rosebud reservations, and Martin is in between the two, a bit further along Highway 18."

Helpfully he pointed to where the dusty macadam disappeared from view.

"Okay, I'll pay them a visit tomorrow, you never can tell."

"Your car, that would be the silver-gray Hyundai with Montana tags?"

I nodded.

"In that case I put the GPS tracker under the right car."

Just like Pater, but at least this one told about it.
"And how about me? How can I track you?"
He shoved a note across the table top, with a phone number on it.
"This one I always have on me, day and night. I'm driving a ten year old GMC pick-up, red with a white cab roof, all four fenders dented."
"No budget?"
He sniggered.
"Just camouflage. Normally I'm more of a classical Ford Mustang kind of guy."
I took another bite, he took another sip of his soda.
"And now?"
He looked at me.
"You keep looking, I keep looking, and we keep each other informed?"
I think I heard that song before…
Oh yeah, almost forgot to tell: as he got up I could see I had been right about the dusty scuffed boots. Sometimes I outdo myself.

* * *

At a sedate speed, enjoying the stunning landscape, I drove back from Pine Ridge to the trading post. Somewhere between Wounded Knee and Manderson my phone buzzed. Curious as always I pulled the disturber of peace and quiet from my chest pocket. I moved the Hyundai off the road, pushed the button with the green horn, and told it who I was.
"Mister Versloos, we have a mutual friend."
I switched off the engine and put the car in "park".

"To whom am I speaking?"
The other side laughed.
"My name won't mean anything to you."
Neither did his accent, I just couldn't place it. It certainly wasn't American, nor Dutch.
"What can I do for you?"
"You are enquiring after your friend Eddy."
"That is correct. Do you know where he is?"
"He, and his wife. I have information for you that will enable you to find them."
I was not really convinced of the good intentions of the unknown stranger. Really not, even.
"I'm listening."
"You know the road to Sharps Corner, where you can make a turn to Kyle. Don't turn, but keep following the road. After a while you'll see Badlands National Park visitors' center, at your left. Are you following me?"
I nodded, and realized how ineffective that was.
"So far, so good."
"The center is at the beginning of a wide dirt road, also to the left. Follow that road. After a few miles you'll reach a bridge across the White Creek. Exactly in the middle of that bridge, under the right side railing, a package of information will be taped to the underside. Follow those to the letter. Make sure you'll be there tomorrow morning at exactly ten o'clock."
I didn't understand, and said so.
"Why don't you just tell me what's going on?"
"Tell me, Mr. Versloos, do you have a beard?"
I took an astonished look at my conversation gadget.
"Um, no, why?"
"Pity, really a pity."

“I really don’t have the faintest idea what you’re talking about.”

But I was only talking to myself. The mysterious stranger had hung up already.

Since I happened to have my talking electronics in my hand, I punched in the number of my new federal friend.

“I didn’t expect to hear from you so soon, Mr. Verslois.”

That was something we had in common. In a few words I told him what the mysterious stranger had ordered me to do.

“Hm, I don’t like it a bit, it smells like a trap.”

Great, how this guy could improve one’s morale so easily.

“Number?”

I pushed the menu button.

“Anonymous.”

“That was to be expected. I will ask to have the call traced, but I’m not expecting a whole lot.”

I hesitated a moment till I posed the next question.

“Am I going there tomorrow?”

“It seems to be the only option. There is a small problem, however. They picked a perfectly deserted spot, it would be noticed if I showed up there, but I’ll try to stay as close as possible.”

I thanked him before I disconnected, but I must admit to having been more at ease.

IV

The next morning I followed Gig Foot Memorial Highway till I found the Badlands visitors' center at my left, at the place where a wide unpaved road met the main road. A sign assured me the sandy road was the Bureau of Indian Affairs Road number 2, and for now I had no reason yet to doubt that. Even the free map I got at Crazy Horse Mountain confirmed it, but naturally I couldn't rule out that everybody was plotting against me. For the moment I trusted nothing and nobody.

The visitors' center was a simple building with steps and a wheelchair ramp to an invitingly closed door. In front was an asphalt parking lot, next to it a larger unpaved one, and a dried out meadow that, judging by the furniture, was intended as a picnic location, marked by an abundance of absent tourists.

The Hyundai was planted on the asphalt in front of a sign informing us that because of the lengthy drought there was an extreme fire danger. Gee, who would have guessed?

Inside it was cool, which explained the closed door. It proved to be a kind of mini-museum, with information on the Lakota and the local nature, and a table with a display of things you shouldn't pick up: mainly fossils and ammunition remnants dating back to when the park was used as a military training ground.

A somewhat elderly and very much sturdily built local man in ranger uniform greeted me, the only visitor, friendly. He proved to be a true fount of information on the area in general and the park in particular. By way of some stuffed animals, a headdress with real eagle feathers and a robe that had once been worn by a buffalo we arrived at a set of wall displays showing how the Indians kept track of their history via a series of drawings, a kind of a cross between a comic strip and steno, I'd say.

It was about time to go to the bridge, as ordered, but first I tried my luck once more with Eddy and Natasja's photographs. No, he was sure he had never seen them, but he didn't mind me posting a copy of the flyer on the bulletin board. I did. I thanked him sincerely and stepped back into the heat.

* * *

It wasn't warm. It wasn't hot. It was an idiotic inhumane inside of an oven on overdrive scorching. According to my tablet it was supposed to be slightly over a hundred local Fahrenheit thingies over here. Measured in the shade. Only there was no shade, only the wide unpaved road leading me ever further into the nothing and nowhere. To my right the Badlands took an ever rougher shape. Thousands, probably millions (I was in a generous mood) of years of erosion had worn the former sea bed into ragged peaks.

As ordered, I stopped at about the right time on the middle of the White Creek bridge. Traffic to hinder was totally lacking, there was not another car in sight. Some maps refer to the White Creek as the White River. They were both lying, nothing was either creeking nor rivering. The stream bed was dry, and cracked by the merciless sun. Some tracks by beasts unknown to me led to a puddle in a bend of the late creek or river – the last trace of water as far as the eye could see. I don't think elephants were among those beasts, I would have recognized those. I think. A few suffering plants were involved in a life-or-death fight over the last few drops of ground water.

Exactly at the middle of the bridge, out of view of the unsuspecting passer-by, a tiny package was taped to the far side of the railing. I ripped it off and a note blinked at the sudden fierce sunlight.

I was supposed to drive west. What is it with Americans and compass points? Why not plain left, straight, right, etc.? As a well-trained Dutchman I had to think for a moment about what was what. West was just plain straight ahead, so why didn't those maroons say so in the first place?

Once more enjoying my air-conditioned driving tin I slowly drove on, whirling up a modestly sized dust cloud behind me. I had thought it had been ragged on my right, but now it really started. Mars couldn't possibly look more inhospitable. To my left undulating dry grassland mixed with deeply worn gullies. Every here and there a dead tree livened up the view. Every here and there something green peeked over the edge of a hollow, a sign there was still some water remaining, or at least had been recently.

I passed a sign indicating the border of the national park, and a building shack for the currently not under way road work.

The road just went on and on into the absolute nothing, up and down, side to side, like a pedigree carnival attraction. Only dryer, and hotter. And dustier, much dustier.

Where were those guys? Where was this road going to end, Wyoming or some other exotic location I didn't know either? I decided not to find out. The other guys obviously weren't here, nobody was here at all besides me. During the last twenty minutes I had counted a grand total of zero cars.

An entrance to a field offered me an opportunity to turn the car, which I gratefully accepted. Calmly I Hyundaied back the other way, so east, according to the natives.

The view really was spectacular, I had never seen anything like it. Leisurely I looked around, and that's why I noticed immediately that my left side view mirror suddenly became demirrored. I heard a bang, and pieces of mirror fluttered away. A quick peek in the still intact other side mirror showed another car appearing out of my cloud of dust, a big dark one, make or model I couldn't tell yet.

What was remarkable were the two arms sticking out of two windows, one on the right and another to the left, both arms ending in hands holding guns. Some more shots were heard, and I heard something ricocheting off the roof. This seemed like a good time to speed up, and I undertook an enthusiastic attempt to push the gas pedal through the floorboard. My Korean friend flew ahead, but so did the motorized gunmen behind me.

With incredible speed I flew along the dirt road, and I'd gladly wager my pursuers and me logging a new local dirt road speed record. Pick-up boys, eat your heart out!

Those guys on my tail must have had radar because they managed to stay close behind me in spite of the by now gigantic dust cloud, and every once in a while I heard a bullet hit the bodywork. Thus far it still was the car's bodywork and not mine, but that could change easily, and I didn't like that prospect at all. My body has the exact amount of openings as prescribed for my model, and if it was up to me I'd keep it that way.

The road work obviously started again, because all of a sudden I noticed an Indian woman sitting on a folding chair on the right shoulder. She held a stop sign that had seen better days. Behind a few strands of barbed wire some horses were wondering what she was doing there.

She was probably completely in her rights with her stop sign, but I really was in no position to comply. With wide open mouth she stared while I flew by with a slightly higher than fast speed. Before I lost sight of her in the dust I noticed her lifting a telephone to her mouth.

Two bends and twenty seconds later I understood the higher purpose of the lady and her sign. From the opposite direction a huge truck appeared. The truck was pulling an even wider low bed trailer. On the trailer was a truly monstrous construction machine, hanging as far over the sides as a proper schnitzel is supposed to hang over the sides of a dinner plate. In front of this gigantic combination rode a brave little pick-up truck with very decorative orange flashing lights, driven by a female pilot who visibly paled. Normally, I'd like to state right now, I have more positive effect on the ladies. Ria will gladly confirm this, as soon as she has recovered from her laughing fit, that is.

I estimated my chances of winning a game of chicken rather low, and I already saw the Hyundai doing an impression of a dead bug on the rapidly approaching bumper. That might really put a dent in my good mood.

Sometimes you just got to follow your instincts. I did, and they led me in a sharp turn to the left, straight through a wooden gate that spontaneously decided to transform in a cloud of splinters, into a meadow. Followed by the stares of three black horses I raced through the rough grassy terrain parallel to the road. Somehow I had intended to get back on the road at the next gate, but some barbed wire across my alternative path disagreed.

I slowed down a bit, but suddenly saw in my mirror that the armed maroons had followed me. Since I already had a lot to explain to Alamo I went down to second gear to get some more traction and once more pushed the gas pedal into the carpet. My Korean flew ahead. I aimed for a rusty iron pole, hoping to flatten it, if I hit the wire between two poles I ran the risk of acquiring the nearest two posts as improvised anchors.

Or so I thought.

Wrongly.

Quite effortlessly the pole was pulled from the ground, and a whole string of adjoining poles joined us. It probably was an interesting view for the road work crew, but it slowed me down enormously. I could almost hear the gunmen laugh as they took up position on my left, well out of reach of my dragged along landscape decorations. All they had to do is wait till I got really stuck.

The Hyundai was getting into trouble, and suddenly a red light illuminated the dashboard. No idea which light it was, but it couldn’t have been good. Willie Nelson said something to me, but no matter how much I appreciate him, I just didn't have any time for him. I was still looking for a gate leading to the road, but it was still hundreds of yards away.

More than a bit worried I looked over my left shoulder at the other car – just in time to see them disappear. One moment they were there, the next they were gone. It took a second and a half to realize that they had ran into one of the many gullies worn into the terrain by rainwater that obviously did fall occasionally after all. Clearly they had been watching me so intently that they forgot to look out for obstacles.

I used the opportunity to stop, and to back up a bit to release the tension of my trusty barbed wire obstacle. Quickly I got out, put the whole collection flat on the ground, and took off again as if the devil was on my tail.

Possibly I could have opened the next gate normally. Maybe not. We'll never know for sure because I accelerated again and splintered the tinder dry wood as easily as its colleague a bit further down. It really didn't make any difference to the paintjob anymore. For a moment I had troubles correcting the fishtailing car, then I raced down the road again, back to what locally passed for civilization.

Still, I remained a gentleman, so when I passed a lady guarding the other side of the stretch of road I waved friendly.

Without slowing down I poured the so necessary remaining contents of my water bottle down my throat. My dust cloud was by now large enough to feed all kind of ill-advised theories on various Google Earth forums. Without slowing down I passed the visitors center, leaving a few millimeters of rubber I pulled onto Big Foot Memorial Highway, heading towards Porcupine.

It took a little while till I realized I was behaving foolishly. My pursuers were swallowed by Mother Earth, the road builders were too flabbergasted to follow me. Luckily there was no traffic, and the only one witnessing how I was making an ass of myself was a deer by the side of the road. I slowed down till the meter mentioned 60.

Before I knew it I was at the Sharps Corner gas station annex convenience store. Only now I noticed I was shaking like a leaf behind the wheel, and I stopped for a cup of diluted ditch water pretending to be coffee. This was not a time to be particular. While I was still contemplating which snack would endanger my health the least Billie White Owl appeared next to me.

"You have no idea of the crazy things that can appear on a screen."

He took a sip of coffee-like water, and didn't twitch a muscle. Typical stoic Indian. Steady as a rock till the bitter end.

"For instance, just a few minutes ago it showed a car driving a while next to a road, as opposed to on it."

I was trying to decipher the chemical composition of something in a colorful package, and was otherwise also in a lousy mood.

"This cowboy could have done with some cavalry, back there."

He shrugged.

"Sorry, only Indians over here, no cavalry. I was too far away, didn't expect that."

"Shouldn't you be fishing those guys out of that canyon and arrest them or something?"

He took another sip, and purely automatically so did I. If I don't get real coffee real soon this lousy country will kill me even before they get another chance at shooting me.

"My superiors would rather know what they're up to. If I arrest them they'll never talk."

I looked at him.

"Maybe I can enlighten you about what they're doing: they were trying to kill me. I'd just as soon not get killed. I want to live to a ripe old age after I populated all of Ommelanderveensloot-Tweededwarsdiep with children, grandchildren and great-grandchildren. I couldn't do that if I were dead, I'm pretty sure of that."

The white owl nodded.

"Yes, I can imagine. But you managed pretty well by yourself, didn't you? You probably don't need me at all."

I've never been this close to hitting a Sicangu FBIan as at that very moment.

"One thing is certain," the agent said, "you're on the right track."

"Excuse me?"

He nodded.

"The fact that they're trying to kill you is evidence you're on to them, they're getting nervous"

"So am I, to be honest. What the hell am I supposed to do now?"

"Two things. First of all, just continue doing whatever it is you are doing, it seems to be working. I'll try to stick a bit closer to you from now on."

"I would appreciate that. And the second thing?"

"Unless you want to go native and keep driving that car as a "rez bomber," you'd better go to Rapid City and get yourself a fresh one."

I scratched behind my ears.

"That is a point. Those people there won't be happy."

To encourage me he patted me on the shoulder.

"See, that is something I can help you with. The Bureau will give them a call and tell them you are working for us. You'll get your car, don't worry."

Still, I was happy I had paid for the collision damage waiver…

* * *

Something buzzed irritatingly. With much trouble I raised an eyelid. 3:55 I saw, in nice red illuminated numbers.

"Nice price," I thought, and turned around.

Half way through the above mentioned turn I heard that irritating buzz again. In the meantime, after a suitable hesitation, a second grey cell had fired up, and was ready for some excitement. The maroon. I picked up my tablet and touch a button imitating spot on the screen. Pater's face appeared. Not something to wake up to, especially not at ridiculous o'clock.

"No," I said to highlight my feelings.

"Good morning, Mr. Versluys. I heard something about an incident yesterday?"

With some well-chosen words, especially considering the hazy time of the day, I explained to him that I didn't consider being shot at as just an incident. He allowed me to rant for about five minutes.

"Ready?"

"May I resume if I think of something else later?"

"By all means. In the meantime I'd like to say that I would understand if you'd want to stop, considering the obvious danger. I know you're going to Rapid City in the morning. I can have a ticket ready and waiting for you at the Delta counter so you can join your wife in Atlanta."

I still wasn't really awake yet, so it took me a full half a second before I explained in colorful detail that I never let my friends down.

Pater nodded.

"To be honest, I hadn't expected anything else. My colleagues assured me they'll keep a better eye on you."

"You do know that your colleagues are represented by, counting all, exactly one person? All right, an original Sicangu with an old pick-up truck, very idyllic, but not really convincing."

He raised his right eyebrow just a little.

"Alone? Is that what he told you? He must have had his reasons, I guess. Between us, he's far from alone, it's just that he's your liaison."

I wondered why White Owl and company judged that secrecy to be necessary, but it was too early and my coffee levels were still too low to concern myself with that.

"Was there anything else? I had planned on sleeping a bit more."

He assured me there was nothing else. With a well-aimed push on a button I put the tablet back to sleep, and turned around to join it. Only the rotten thing woke me again an hour later…

Okay, this time it wasn't so bad, this time it was Ria, who had momentarily forgotten about the two hour time difference between Atlanta and this side of South Dakota. Yes, this side, because the line between two time zones runs through the middle of the state. Have I cited Asterix yet? About them being crazy over here? I could not imagine having to reset my watch every time I passed Amersfoort. Or would experienced Mid-South-Dakotans just have two, watches I mean, one for each wrist? To be honest, I wasn't really sure I wanted to know.

Ria was much more enthusiastic than I was, but then she was awake already. Perhaps she'd even had coffee already? No, no dirty words, she was way too sweet for that, in spite of her demonstrating her caffeinated advantage. She told me that she finished her work in Atlanta sooner than expected and that she was about to get on a plane that would take her via New York and Minneapolis to Rapid City. Could I pick her up?

Oh yes, I could. She thought that was so sweet that I decided not to tell her yet why I had to be in Rapid City anyhow.

"Did you find out anything already?"

She knew better than that, she knew perfectly well I would have called her immediately.

"I have an FBI acquaintance who would answer to that that we are listening to all signals, so we can better coordinate our search."

She sighed.

"Colleague of Pater's?"

"Undeniable. Would you mind if I go and try to catch another hour of sleep? You do want me to be well rested for you, don't you?"

In reply she said something she couldn't possibly have meant, and the screen went back to sleep.
So did both of my grey cells.

* * *

Since I now had all morning, I took my time for coffee, breakfast, coffee, checking my mail, coffee, checking the news, and some coffee. By nine I got into my abused set of wheels. Sedately I drove right from the trading post's gate, along the lousy but scenic road, till it met Big Foot Memorial Highway, where I took a left, or North, as it is expressed locally. Because of the international relations once in while one has to howl with the wolves, but you and I know darn well I was just heading to Rapid City.
As I passed the ranger station where the dirt road began where I had raced those fateful kilometers, or, if you're so inclined, miles I wondered if the car would still be stuck in that gully. Automatically I checked my remaining two mirrors, but there was not a soul behind me.
Yesterday I had been impressed by the scenery along the side road, but here it wasn't bad at all either. Unimaginable spectacular valleys alternated with wide open prairie, with again those odd little hillocks.
Sadly I had to pay a lot of attention to the road, since here also animals were looking for the last remaining grass on the verge. A deer stared at me with huge eyes as I zapped by her or him at a hair's breadth distance, I'm sorry it was all a bit too fast to check which of the two it was, nor did I really care, so please stop asking me things that have nothing to do with the story but only distract

me, maroon, but a palomino obviously had seen it all before and grazed along cold bloodedly.

All in all it was just over an hour and a half from the trading post to the airport but I wasn't bored for a single minute of it.

I passed the turn off for the airport, since I still had to fill the tank. Chances are they wouldn't blame me if I returned the wreck with its tank only half full, but a deal was a deal, and Pater was paying anyhow. A handful of kilometermileminutes later, at the edge of Rapid City, I found a gas station.

Once filled up I drove back the few klicks to the airport entrance. Signs directed me to the right parking lot. I parked neatly in the correct row, and memorized the number of the spot itself – as if they could possibly mistake this car for any other in the lot…

It was quiet, only one other customer was ahead of me at the Alamo desk. The manager had already spotted me, and bounced out of her cubicle. She didn't really look happily at the key and the documents I deposited in front of her on the counter.

"You had some damage, I understand. How bad is it?"

She handed me a damage form, with views of all sides of a generic vehicle.

"Could you indicate approximately where?"

I accepted her pen and crosshatched front and sides. At the rear I drew some little stars to indicate bullet holes, and some lines on the roof to mark ricochets. Very decidedly I crossed out the late wing mirror.

When she looked at me again it was much less friendly.

"Are you sure that's everything?"

"The radio is still fine."

It didn't make her laugh. She put some papers in front of me.

"Please sign here, here, here and here."

I signed there, there, there and there. She put the papers away carefully, and for just this once I would almost feel sorry for the insurance company.

Almost.

Like, not.

She handed me a new folder of documents, and keys.

"Would you mind not damaging this one?"

"I'll try my very best."

She shook her head.

"Would you mind if I came along with you to the parking lot? I'd like to inspect the damage myself, and your new car is there as well."

I didn't mind, and she came along. She sighed theatrically when she saw what had been done to her almost brand new Hyundai, and shook her undoubtedly wise head.

"If the FBI hadn't called I'd not be too sure if I'd have given you a replacement car."

But they had, and she did. It turned out to be a twin brother to my first Hyundai, same model, same color, only this time with South Dakota tags. I shook her hand, she shook her head, and I drove away before she could change her mind.

There were still a few hours to kill, so I decided to drive into town and do some shopping and snacking.

Shopped and snacked I returned well in time. Just to be on the safe side I avoided the Alamo desk and entered the terminal building via another entrance.

In the main hall a primitive historical airplane was hanging suspended from the ceiling. As a young boy I built quite a few plastic model planes, and hung them by threads from my bedroom ceiling. Once in a while one of them spontaneously crashed down, and after dusting off that memory and putting it back in a safe spot I decided to make a respectful detour around this adult version. To be fair I have to admit I heard no sounds of a crash, so my precautions may have been superfluous – this time.

Ria was part of the herd of passengers coming out of the exit gate. She saw me, and flew into my arms. The rest of the herd failed to follow her example but neither of us really minded.

"I'm so glad to see you again! Any news yet on Eddy and Natasja?"

I shook my head, and as we strolled to the luggage carrousel I reviewed what had happened so far for her. Worriedly she looked me over to check I wasn't injured.

"And that FBI agent, he really doesn't know?"

"No, I believe him when he says he doesn't. His idea of a gang looking for a quiet place to do their business doesn't sound all that unlikely, but I don't understand them attracting attention by kidnapping Eddy and Natasja. We're still missing a lot of puzzle pieces."

"And what are we to do now?"

I raised my shoulders.

"There are a few more businesses in Pine Ridge that I want to visit with our posters, we'll do that tomorrow morning, in the afternoon we can go to the newspaper office, in Martin. Perhaps we can do a bit more afterwards at that side of the reservation, I haven't been there at all yet."

After a few minutes wait her suitcase rolled through the hatch on the conveyor belt. Always the gentleman, I dragged it for her to the car. I didn't have to drag Ria, she came on her own accord.

Not totally unexpectedly Ria had a good time taking in the sights to and for me back to the trading post. Susie received her friendly, and presented us with a delicious meal

We both checked our mail, and after that neither of us needed many words to agree on withdrawing to our room.

When I'm asleep I'm asleep, and very little will wake me. Alarm clocks, telephones, Ria's elbow, yes, they will do the job all the time, but odors? No, not really. Which only goes to prove that the sickly sweet smell of decay floating in through the window screen was not an odor but a true stench. While Ria was making unamused sounds I shut the window and opened the door to get at least some breathable air.

Quite guilelessly Susie told us the next morning that during the night one of the dogs had lost a discussion with a stunk. I had a dark brown feeling it had been the large white one who usually sleeps on the landing under our bedroom window. It also became clear to me why the Dutch word for skunk literally translates as "stink animal".

V

That morning Ria and I went to Pine Ridge to distribute some more of my mini-posters. You never can tell. Ria wanted to do some shopping while we were there, and by lack of alternatives the Sioux Nation supermarket became our target.

I pulled into the driveway next to the Mexican place, onto the supermarket parking lot, and found a parking space sadly lacking in shade. We pulled a shopping cart from the row, and shoved it into the store.

Ria noticed right away that her brand of carbonated brown water was well represented. I decided to live a little while longer and not mention the local diabetes statistics – the highest in the country.

Being a good housewife Ria started comparing prices right away, and voiced her surprise of the lack of listings of E-numbers and other additives.

The prices just made her shake her head. And we thought we were getting screwed in the Netherlands!

All of a sudden I stood eye to eye with somebody I knew, and who looked as surprised as I probably did.

"Wij kennen elkaar!" ("We know each other") I said in Dutch.

Ria gave me a look indicating that I had to be careful talking to strange women in her presence, especially if I wanted to keep all of my body parts in working order.

"Ria, this is the lady I told you about, who is running the Wildervank Buddhist center."

"Ankie," she introduced herself to Ria, who in return told her name.

Something puzzled me.

"But how does somebody from the far Wildervank end up in Pine Ridge?"

There was that broad smile again I remembered so well.

"I just took part in a Buddhist congress in Boulder, Colorado. I flew in via Denver, but since I have heard so much about Pine Ridge from Gerrit and Candy, and I loved their pictures, I decided to pass through here on my way back, and fly back via Rapid City."

"Gerrit and Candy are the Postmas, the people in Veendam who helped me with background information for my article."

This in reply to Ria's puzzled look.

"Did you get to see a lot over here already?"

Ankie shook her head.

"I've just arrived and now I'm doing some shopping before I go on."

She fished a note from a pocket.

"From here I'll be going to Wounded Knee, and from there to a bed and breakfast near Sharpe's Corner. I also plan to visit the Badlands as well, and the college."

We assured her there was plenty to see.

"And how is your article coming along?"

I nodded.

"I've been collecting so much material that it will probably turn into a series of articles."

We exchanged some more information about various unimportant stuff, and said our goodbyes at the parking lot.

* * *

That bloody thing in my chest pocket disturbed me half way through a burrito at the Mexican place on the main road. Amused, Ria watched how I tried not to choke before I at least had said my name. It took a large sip of soda, but in the end I succeeded

"Wim, Billie White Owl. Perhaps we've located your friends. There's a fire just beyond Potato Creek, and somebody told Tribal Police they had seen some strangers."

I jumped up.

"How do I get there?"

At that moment two red pickup trucks screamed by, decorated with flashing lights.

"Never mind, I've got an escort."

Followed by the stupefied gazes of our fellow eaters I ran out, Ria on my heels. We jumped into the Hyundai, in spite of the rush neatly each on one side, old habits die hard, and raced after the firemen, generously spraying gravel on neighboring tin.

"May I know where we're going?"

"To the fire. Billie thinks Eddy may be involved with it somehow."

Ria clicked shut her safety belt, and in spite or possibly because of our speed I did so too, without removing my foot from the gas pedal, since I didn't want to lose our guides. With un-American speed we sped down highway 18, and with screaming tires we took the turn-off to Wounded Knee.

Luckily our fellow road users dove well-disciplined in their respective verges to clear the road for our red leaders, and we followed thankfully in their wake.

Full compliments for Ria, she didn't utter a word, but I saw the knuckles of the hand gripping the door handle turn whiter and whiter.

At Sharps Corner I almost lost control of the car when I slipped on some sand at the turn-off to Kyle but I could correct before we found out if there was a ditch hiding under the weeds next to the road making plastic surgery a necessity for this Hyundai as well. Over the hills we continued, past the motel and the college, through Kyle proper, where the store visitors had ran out to watch the spectacle. In my mirrors I saw some cars joining our parade.

"Look!" Ria exclaimed, and pointed to a column of black smoke on the horizon to our left.

A mile or so after crossing the stream that gave Potato Creek its name the fire trucks took a left, so we did too. A low ridge prevented us from seeing the exact location of the fire. A right into an unpaved road, the fire trucks were now shrouded in dense dust clouds. So were we probably, I didn't have time or inclination to check my mirror.

* * *

After crossing the last rise it became clear what was the source of the boiling black mass of smoke. An old trailer was on fire, and the flames had jumped to an adjoining shed. The two fire department pick-ups stopped, the crew jumped out, and within a minute two in my inexperienced eyes totally inadequate streams of water tried in vain to extinguish the fire.

We jumped out of Hyundai II but were stopped by a Tribal Police officer when we got too close.

"Careful, there's a gas tank behind the house."

At that precise moment an explosion confirmed the former presence of the afore mentioned tank. Ria and I ducked down, but nothing flew in traditional Hollywood style over our heads.

"Do you think they were in there?" Ria asked. I had been wondering the same.

"Probably not," I said, mainly to improve my own morale.

Ria rubbed her eyes, even though the wind blew the smoke the other way.

I asked the officer.

"Do you know if there was anybody inside?"

He shrugged.

"Nobody seems to know anything. Some say there were two strangers hanging around here, a man and a woman. The owner is not here, Jimmie Spotted Horse is still serving another year. As you can see there are no immediate neighbors, so nobody can say for sure if there really were people here recently. We're trying to get a hold of the family, but they seem to be in Wanblee."

All of a sudden Billie White Owl was standing next to us.

"Great spot to do something nobody is supposed to know anything about."

I looked at him.

"Do you think…?"

He shrugged his shoulders.

"Everything is possible, nothing is certain."

A bit curter than was strictly necessary I thanked him for that remarkable insight. In the meantime all that remained of the trailer were some ashes and a few remnant on a heat twisted frame. I couldn't bear the thought that Eddy and…

"Wow, not much left there," I heard a voice behind me.

I turned around, and stood eye in eye with a grinning Eddy, and a brightly smiling Natasja who had wrapped herself around his arm. Both were covered in soot.

"Eddy! Where the hell did you come from all of a sudden?"

Natasja embraced me.

"Cuba libre!"

Long story, but we met when she was serving me that particular drink, a number of years ago. Even I cannot live by coffee alone.

"Quiet," I grinned, "alcohol isn't allowed here!"

The local audience observed in amazement our smoky group hug. It took a while before Eddy and I could liberate ourselves from our better halves, who by lack of alternatives fell crying into each other's arms. An elderly lady draped a totally superfluous blanket over Natasja's shoulders and handed her a bottle of water, with a gratefully accepted hug.

"Sorry for the theatrics, but I didn't have a mobile phone handy, and I figured this would attract attention. I guess it did."

He made a wide gesture encompassing firemen, police and the still increasing audience.

There was a discrete cough next to me.

"Eddy, Billie White Owl, a three lettered acronym friend of Pater's. Billie, Eddy Kamminga, village idiot."

The owl and the village idiot shook each other's front paws.

"Could you spare a moment of your time for me? I would like some explanation about what happened recently."

We looked at the crowd surrounding us.

"Perhaps it would be smarter to go to the trading post. Over there they have privacy and reasonably good coffee."

Eddy and I ambled over to Ria and Natasja.

"Coffee at Susie's, and catch up a bit?"

And after a look at the soot-covered Natasja.

"There's a bathroom there as well."

Natasja looked at White Owl.

"Can we make a stop at our hotel to pick up some clothes?"

He shrugged.

"Hop in my truck."

The Tribal Police officer wanted to talk with Billie, but he whispered something that obviously killed the curiosity instantly.

Eddy and Natasja climbed into the cab of White Owl's truck, we followed in our car, back through Kyle, where the onlookers had returned to doing whatever they had been doing before, to the motel.

Billie asked us to wait in the lobby while he informed the front desk that the disapearees had reappeared and needed a room key. While a modest mob of hotel people started gossiping behind the counter, Billy accompanied Eddy and Natasja, he wanted to make sure there was no uninvited company in their room. Ria was too excited to be really interested in the offered souvenirs while I browsed through the folder rack without actually seeing something.

As I looked for the fourhundredandthirtysecond time if they were coming, it actually happened. Eddy carried his own suitcase, Natasja was employing Billie for the heavy work.

Across the by now familiar hills, left at Sharps Corner, right at a burned meadow into Gooseneck Road, more hills, right, and the Dancing Pony trading post.

Susie and her crew were already standing on the porch, waiting for us, so I guessed the smoke signals were still working fine. I introduced our friends, and asked if the second room was still vacant. Smiling she informed me that Billie White Owl had already reserved it for them.

We dragged the suitcases up the outside staircase, Susie showed them their room and Natasja the bathroom, she pointed at a large pot of coffee, and began improvising a hot meal.

* * *

The four of us plus Billie White Owl were seated at the long table in the trading post, enjoying Susie's coffee. Natasja had quickly freshened herself up a bit in our bathroom, Eddy was still aromatic.

Unusually shy Eddy looked at Billie, Ria and me.

"I must admit that I never realized what our temporary disappearance would unleash. I'm sorry to have made you worry more than necessary."

My thoughts went to the last and now late Hyundai, according to me those worries were not that unfounded.

"You know him better than me, has he been a pyromaniac for a long time?"

I shook my head, people consider it not done shaking somebody else's, unless previously agreed and with properly washed hands, naturally.

"I've known him way too long, but as far as I know this was a first, besides some ill-fated chemical experiments"

White Owl now aimed his arrows at Eddy.

"Okay, so you're not a pyromaniac. Why then did you burn down that trailer? Because it was you, you admitted that already."

Eddy nodded. As a good friend he aped my behavior, and also used his own head.

"I didn't bring my cell phone."

According to Hollywood at least Indians are supposed to be imperturbable. The same goes for FBI agents. Still, our owl had an odd look on his face.

"Beg pardon?"

Eddy coughed the last bits of soot out of his longs, and cleared his throat.

"Perhaps it would be best if I start at the beginning."

"Well, we might as well give it a try."

"As you all know, I was invited by my colleague Mike Two Horses to have a look at the local polluted drinking water. We had met a few years ago at a congress on soil pollution, where I reported on my bacteriological soil regeneration experiments. The drinking water is just plain poisonous, many elders have to get dialysis because their kidneys just can't cope with it anymore. Two Horses remembered my presentation, and hoped we could use my bacteria here as well. By the way, we couldn't, as my very first test already showed, but I figured we could do something with reverse osmosis."

Our federal friend looked at me.

"Could you translate, please?"

"Just nod, smile, and pretend you're getting it, that's what Ria and I usually do."

Eddy gave us that look he usually reserved for normal plain mortals, and continued.

"Two Horses allowed me the use of a modest corner of the college laboratory, and I built a trial installation."

"Did it work?" I enquired in pure innocence. A destructive look was the immediate reply.

"Of course it worked, it's a very simple process. And to explain it simply, in other words especially for you, Wim, it is like an ultrafine filtering system, but at a molecular level. The problem was that it couldn't be used over here. We couldn't build an installation large enough for the complete water supply, that would be way too large and way too expensive. After much brainstorming we figured it should be possible to develop a simple and cheap compact installation that could be put in each individual house. It would at least clean the drinking and cooking water, for water used for laundry for instance it wouldn't make a difference anyhow."

I still didn't see how this was leading to their disappearance from their hotel and to the burning trailer. What I did know is that that there was no way you could hurry Eddy, best to let him follow his own tread at leisure. The maroon.

"We were at a stage that we could move from the tests to a production model. It had to be simple, cheap and compact. We managed to find a shipment of cheap leftover housings and were trying to fold all the components into it. Then the phone call came."

He took a sip, I'm certain more for the theatrical effect than because of thirst. Yes, the maroon.

"Somebody with an odd accent said that he had a nice proposition for me. He had a recipe, and he wanted me to build a professional installation for him. Naturally I understood this to be about synthetic drugs, but I told him to check the Yellow Pages for installation builders, and hung up on him. He called back immediately to tell me he didn't like that. He also mentioned an amount."

He looked at Billie.

"A million dollars. I hung up again. That evening somebody mailed me some pictures. They had followed Natasja and wanted to demonstrate how vulnerable she was. We conferred, and decided to disappear. Purely coincidentally we knew about that trailer, it belonged to an acquaintance of one of the lab people. We drove to the Chadron, Nebraska, Walmart, because there our looks were a bit more common than over here, loaded the car with canned and other preserved food and bottled water, and as soon as it got dark we went to the trailer."

"Two questions," White Owl interrupted. "Did you have a key to the trailer, and what did you do with the car?"

"One: no, but a good pocket knife. Two: a few hundred yards from the trailer, under a tarp and some bushes and stuff. Perhaps we should pick it up one of these days, the rental place would probably like that."

Well, I thought, they are getting used to a lot of things lately…

"It is quite bizarre, you know, out there in the middle of nowhere, without gas, electricity, sewer, phone, internet, totally nothing." He blinked at Natasja. "Not that we didn't manage to entertain ourselves."

She blushed a decent bit.

"We had no idea how long we still had to stay there, but our supplies would last at least another week, after that we'd take a careful look if the air had cleared. But then they appeared, all of a sudden."

Billie couldn't control his impatience anymore.

"Who? How? Where?"

"Once in a while we went out to get some fresh air. You have seen for yourself that there is not a living soul around there, so we figured we could do so safely. Yesterday we saw a big black car methodically entering one side road after another. There were two people in it. Because of the distance we couldn't determine who or what, but we knew it was trouble. They were still some distance away, but it was only a matter of time till they would find us. There was nowhere to run, so we decided to call for help if they came to us. As you both know we didn't have our phones on us but since everybody is very nervous about fires around here at the moment that seemed to be the best solution. As soon as they entered our road Natasja hid in a ditch, and I put the trailer on fire, and joined her to wait till help showed up. The rest you know."

Our own private special agent shook his head.

"I'm relieved the riddle of your disappearance turned out to be a lot of nothing, but I'm still a bit worried the gang from which you were hiding suddenly disappeared into thin air. To be honest I'd rather stick around a while longer, but that would probably be deemed unnecessary by higher powers."

While Billie occupied Eddy with some questions to fill in the final details I called Pater who, I assumed, would still be anxious to learn what happened.

"That is good news, but just like special agent White Owl I'm not totally at ease that the gang would have given up this easily. Tell your federal friend that I'm asking his superiors for further investigation and a proper risk assessment."

"So you don't think they're safe now?"

He thought for a moment.

"I'm not sure at all about anything, I'd rather be careful for a while longer."

In the meantime White Owl was through with Eddy who disappeared into the shower, to the great relief of all others present.

Once deEddyfied Billy retreated to the outside stairs with his phone and a mug of coffee, out of earshot of the others. Once the mug was finished he came back inside and poured himself a fresh one. Someone who drinks that much coffee has to be one of the good ones.

"I don't know if you'll consider this to be good news or bad, but I'll continue keeping you company. My superiors want me to keep an eye of you till we are sure the gangsters really disappeared."

Susie had a worried look on her face.

"I only have the two rooms up here, and they're both taken now. There are more sleeping places across the yard, but they're not as comfortable."

The owl shook his head.

"That couch looks comfortable enough."

She shrugged, and probably thought of Asterix too.

The next morning, right before lunch, White Owl received another phone call. Again he retreated with his mobile talking contraption to the outside stairs. After a few minutes he returned, a wide smile on his face.

"You are rid of me after all, people. That was my bureau chief. Three cars with, as far as we can be sure, the gang members rode into Nebraska, and from there to Wyoming. It looks like they gave up and ran. My supporting team has been withdrawn already, and now I'm leaving you as well."

For a final time we sat down around the long table.

"It's a pity we didn't get them here, but now that they're in our sights there's a good chance we will eventually. We know what they want, and we do have some idea who they are."

Everybody kept their silence pensively, I just hope the others pensitated more positively than I did.

"I really feel lousy about setting fire to that trailer," Eddy said, "but I didn't see any other options to attract attention. A smoke signal, yes."

Nobody laughed, so he refrained himself as well.

"If the insurance doesn't pay, naturally I'll be good for any and all damages."

Billie nodded.

"I'll have it looked into, I'll get back to you on that."

He took a sip.

"Good coffee."

"So, now back to....?" I couldn't help myself asking.

"First I'll spend a few days with my relatives in Mission, after that I'll be heading back to our district offices in Pierre."

"Let's hope not, but should something happen?"

"You got my number, I always have that phone with me. Should that not work for whatever reason you can always call the Pierre office. We're in the book, under F."

After the ritualistic shaking of extremities he left us.

"So now?" I asked when the four of us were sitting together once more on the huge L-shaped couch. Eddy was the first to react.

"My vacation is almost finished. Tomorrow I'd like to see Two Horses, I think he can take charge of the project by now, and otherwise there still is e-mail. Do you have some time left, so we can hang out here for say a week?"

Ria was already nodding enthusiastically, and I happily joined in. Natasja was almost literally glowing because of this prospect.

* * *

The next morning we returned to Potato Creek, in a much happier mood than the previous day, to pick up Eddy's car. On the dusty sportsground of the Kyle school some boys were listlessly throwing baseballs to each other. Passing the for this area abundant but to me totally unknown trees we drove on to Potato Creek. Soon we reached the source of Eddy's smoke signals.

We got out, stretched, and cast an eye on the remains of trailer and shed.

"I don't like destroying stuff, but this time I saw no other way."

I patted him on the shoulder and followed him into a field. Behind some large bushes was a large pile of junk.

Eddy started pulling branches from it, and since I had nothing else to do, I helped him. We revealed a grey tarpaulin that we pulled aside together. A large silver-gray car spontaneously glistened in the bright sunlight and Eddy looked as happy as a little child

* * *

We were still in a party mood when the four of us entered the Pine Ridge Sioux Nation supermarket. Besides the usual soft drinks and snacks Ria and Natasja wanted to take a look at the modest souvenirs section. With two fully laden shopping carts we got to the check out, where the young lady who knew darn well we were strangers – except for the store manager we were the only non-natives in the whole store – inquired if we had a steady customers loyalty card.

As we were stuffing everything in our vehicles' trunks – why did the maroon happen to have a full size Nissan when I had to do with a totally adequate but much more modest Hyundai? – a guy in a motorized wheelchair, a painting in his lap, came to bother us. He flattened several of my toes as he forced his way in between us, and distracted because of that I didn't even see the blue delivery van coming.

All of a sudden we heard a scream, and we caught a glimpse of Natasja being pulled in the open sliding side door. Even before the door was properly closed the car took off with screeching tires. It raced by the astounded visitors of the food bank at the end of the parking lot, and disappeared around the corner of that building.

We managed to wrestle ourselves free of the pushy wheelchair pilot, and jumped in our respective cars. We didn't get very far – both cars had a flat front tire.

Ria and I looked at each other, and I grabbed my mobile from my chest pocket.

"Billie White Owl? I hate to tell you, but I fear your vacation is over…"

In the meantime Eddy entertained himself by producing an extremely creatively selected series of combinations of adjectives and nouns. I think I noted the odd adverb in the mix but this was neither the place nor the time to go all grammarly on him.

VI

I noted on the site of the American foundation that was working together with the Veendam folks of Cosmic Fire Foundation, that the next day would be a food distribution day. That meant we had to hurry. The ladies downstairs at the trading post always knew everything, so they also knew exactly where Jeff Slaughter's building was located. Jeff was the man responsible for the whole food program. The building happened to be a warehouse near the airfield. A convenience store on highway 18 was the easiest recognizable landmark. For a moment I considered calling ahead, but I didn't see what that would add. Eddy didn't care, as long as we hurried up.

Considering the local sensitivities we decided to inform Billie but not take him along. He advised us by phone he understood.

At ridiculous o'clock the next morning we got up, fixed ourselves some sandwiches and an abundance of coffee, and got under way. There was hardly any traffic, I doubt we saw as many as ten cars before we got to Pine Ridge. I saw the "closed" signs at the convenience store, and drove on to the paint starved warehouse some way behind it. The large main door was still closed, but a smaller door beside it was invitingly open. I parked the car on a spot that I hoped was in nobody's way and entered through a small hallway.

A bear shaped man was stirring in a large pan. He looked up, and smiled friendly.

"Soup is ready, or would you prefer coffee?"

“Coffee,” I said, and got some. Eddy joined me, Ria sampled the soup and made appreciating sounds after the first slurp. The coffee wasn’t half bad either. Gratefully sipping the hot liquid I looked around me. Still empty trestle tables were set up in the large open space, in the back I noticed some large freezers. Banners and posters on mainly sports and music covered the walls.

“I was already wondering when I was going to meet you,” the stirring bear remarked.

It doesn’t happen too often, but now I was truly surprised.

“You know who we are?”

He grinned.

“Wim Versloowees. Together with your friend and your wife you’re searching for Natasja. I am Jeff Slaughter, as you must have figured by now.”

My astonished face must have been something to behold.

“Candy mailed me already that you’d be in the neighborhood, and that she had told you about me. You have been asking about Eddy and Natasja everywhere: at Kyle College, all over Pine Ridge, at the Manderson store, at the park ranger’s, you name it. Then there was that fire near Potato Creek, and I heard something about a kidnapping. Stuff like that doesn’t happen every day around here. What I don’t get is why Candy Postma had the impression you were a journalist.”

I nodded, by now also grinning.

“I do know how to write, and I hate long explanations.”

He nodded, both of us took a sip.

“What do you think I can do for you, Wim?”

I told him, and he nodded.

“The first ones will be arriving any moment. When they’re all here I’ll have a word with them.”

He took another sip, and replenished our mugs.

“By the way, at the newspaper nobody knew anything either.”

My expression must have spoken for itself once more.

“Didn’t they tell you I’m a regular contributor to the Lakota Country Times? I asked the people I know there if they knew anything more about this, but nobody knew anything, as I said.”

I looked with fresh appreciation at Jeff. This man knew how to get things going! Even Eddy perked up a bit, so extra points for that.

“If she’s still on the reservation we’ll find her, I can guarantee that.”

A bit later the first drivers entered, and everybody helped themselves to coffee and soup. The all eyed us curiously, but besides friendly greetings nobody said anything. We had no idea if they already knew who we were, or if they were just waiting till somebody informed them.

That happened when everybody was present. Jeff got up, and right away the chatting died away.

“These people are from the Netherlands, they are friends of people who are paying for part of our food parcels. Eddy over there is working with the Kyle College to find a way to make our drinking water safe again. Now they need our help. Natasja, Eddy’s wife, has been kidnapped by a gang, to blackmail him. They are asking us to keep our eyes open, and to ask around if anybody has seen anything unusual.

He pointed at my modest little stack of remaining posters.
"Take one of these, then you have our picture and Wim's phone number. Don't bother looking for Eddy, that's him over there."
Laughter all around. Somebody asked something in Lakota.
"No, absolutely not! Don't do anything, don't let anybody notice what you saw. Just call either Wim or me."
There were a few more questions, but they were more to seek confirmation on one point or another. Our coffee and soup session came to an abrupt end when a truck arrived to deliver supplies. The large door went up, and the semi's trailer was backed up into the building. Jeff put everybody to work unloading everything and dividing it over well over five hundred food boxes – we were drafted as well, and didn't mind a bit. It took our minds of other stuff for a while.

* * *

Something stirred in my chest pocket. It didn't hurt, tickle, nor irritate in any other way, but out of undiluted curiosity I pulled it out anyway. Eddy and me were at that time sitting at the by now well-known long table while Ria was trying to understand how Susie's vegetable desiccator functioned, and how badly we needed one.
"Wim Versluys," I said, thus indicating to any good listener that I was willing to communicate. A not unknown voice replied.

"Ah, Mr. Versloos, I'm so pleased to hear you again!"

Personally I was much less pleased, and indicated so subtly.

"Not due to a lack of trying by you, your goons almost blasted me to the eternal hunting grounds."

Soft laughter at the other side.

"Well, I had to try something, didn't I? I thought at the time you were in the way, but that passed by itself. But we're still friends, right? Believe me, right now I'm not planning to hurt you in any way."

Eddy came closer, a question in his facial expression. I gestured him to be silent.

"Where is Natasja? I demand her immediate release."

Again that irritating laughter.

"Mrs. Kamminga is well, just a pity she's not impressed by my considerable charms. And her being my type and all – female, you know."

"What do you want?"

"You know very well what I want, I need to borrow Mr. Kamminga for a few months. He has to start up production for us. As soon as that is running and he has trained people to keep it running, I have no further interest in him."

Which was not quite the same as not killing him, I noticed as an unspoken aside.

"Before we continue this conversation, I want to make sure Natasja is in good shape. I want her on the phone."

A short irritation.

"I don't think so, Mr. Versloos."

"In that case it's senseless to talk on."

I pushed the button with the red phone. Eddy looked at me as if I had gone crazy.

“What are you doing, you idiot?”

“Without a sign of life we’re not doing anything. Call White Owl from your phone, will you? I want to keep this one free, I’m expecting a call any moment now.”

Correct, at that precise moment sound and light indicated somebody not being able to live without me anymore.

“Are you sure you don’t have a beard? You do behave as if you have one.”

“Where is Natasja?”

“I’ll call you again at four o’clock exactly, so Mr. Kamminga and you may convince yourselves that she’s doing well. For now, at least.”

This time he was the red phone button pusher. I saw Eddy putting his phone away.

“White Owl is coming.”

Half an hour later the familiar beat-up pick-up was parked in front of the trading post and White Owl was sitting at the table with us, his hands warming around a mug of Susie’s acceptable coffee. He peeked at a wristwatch that actually looked way too good to fit with his outfit.

“Another hour.”

“I’m not very technically inclined,” I confessed, “but shouldn’t it be possible to trace the call back to where he is now?”

“That was kind of tricky already when we were just dealing with only land lines, most experienced criminals knew that they shouldn’t talk too long. With mobiles it’s a lot more difficult. If we’re lucky we’ll find out what cell tower he was in the vicinity of, but that's still a pretty big vicinity."

"Well, shouldn't you be warning somebody anyhow? That they keep an eye on things or so?"

He smiled.

"Your telephone is already being monitored ever since Natasja's disappearance, as well as Eddy's and Ria's, and even the trading post's land line is enjoying our undivided attention."

"Sorry, I wasn't thinking, I should have known better."

"If it's any consolation, we haven't had your conversations with Ria translated, so at least we left you with you with that much privacy."

Don't forget, there are still people out there who believe that Americans don't understand irony…

"I'm leaving now, I'm afraid they might be watching the trading post. Call me as soon as the call is over."

I could say the hour flew by, but I wouldn't be speaking the truth. Susie probably had to refinish the section of the floor where Eddy's walking had worn through four coats of varnish. We were all as tightly wound as possible, and all three of us jumped up when the phone rang, exactly on time.

"Wim Versluys."

"Good afternoon, Mr. Versloos. There's a lady here with me who would like to speak with Mr. Kamminga."

Without a word I handed Eddy the contraption.

"Natasja, are you there?" he bellowed into the poor thing. Obviously the answer was confirmative because he changed to caring little sounds. That went on for about two minutes, then all of a sudden he looked sad, and handed me the still smoking phone.

"He wants to talk to you."

The other side confirmed this immediately.

"Ah, Mr. Versloos, good to hear you again. I'm assuming your friend is too emotional to make a proper deal right now."

"What do you want?"

I heard some digitally transferred soft laughter.

"You know already what I want, I want to borrow Mr. Kamminga for a few months."

"You mean, you want to trade him against his wife."

"No, that's not what I had in mind, not right now, at least. As soon as Kamminga is with me, and commences working, then I'll let her go, not a minute sooner."

I didn't believe him, and said so.

"Ah, my beardless friend, it doesn't matter whether you believe me or not, this is how it's going to happen anyhow. I understand you're not very familiar with the area, so let's select an easily recognizable meeting point. Tomorrow morning at nine o'clock, at the Wounded Knee cemetery, at the top of the hill. Do I have to tell you that if I even as much as smell police I will have a body part of Mrs. Kamminga removed? The mail is rather slow around here, so it might be a few days till you receive it at the trading post."

Any attempt to answer was totally superfluous, my mobile was already trying to catch its breath disconnectedly in my hand.

Eddy looked at me desperately.

"That got us nowhere, that way he'll have both of us in his power."

I agreed with him, but to preserve the troops' morale I decided to keep my mouth shut.

"It will all work out, believe me."

That believing bit, I might have to work on that a bit myself.

* * *

I called Billie White Owl to inform him of Natasja's kidnappers' message. Totally superfluous, he had been listening along. We agreed to meet at the Pine Ridge Subway.

My sandwich with among other components a fair amount of dead pig had hardly been constructed as he came in. He ordered something as well, and joined me at a table.

"Okay, your ideas," he said after his first bite.

I took a sip of my soda – caution prevented me from trying the coffee – and started.

He didn't interrupt me, allowed me to finish at length.

"I don't like that spot in the least. He is assuming we are here, and he's playing a game with us."

"Please explain?"

He didn't look overjoyed.

"You know what happened at Wounded Knee, not just in 1890, but also in 1973?"

I knew.

"Then you will understand that any federal presence there might have far reaching consequences, and I don't want that on my conscience."

"So you think that's why they picked that precise spot?"

He nodded and took another bite.

"I'm convinced of it. Besides that, there are three roads you can take from there, and from the cemetery hill you can keep an eye on all three of them."

I nodded.

"Yes, I remember that."

He thought for a moment.

"I'll have to contact my superiors, this is way above my pay grade. If something goes wrong here, it might be very wrong."

"And you're not worried they'll just charge in with a lot of show of force? If those guys suspect just anything they could really start returning Natasja in little pieces. Do you really think they can stay in the background as long as is necessary? Do you really think they would be able to, if they wanted to?"

White Owl chewed pensively.

"That might indeed be a bit of a challenge."

A sip.

"I can only see one path of action, and that is calling my special agent in charge. He'll have to help me figure out what to do."

He shoved the remainder of his sandwich into his head and took his beverage along outside. I saw him getting into his car and taking to his phone. Every once in a while the thing replied, as could be derived from the pauses at this side. I couldn't really say he was looking much happier. After a while he put the machine away and came back inside.

"So?"

A perfectly executed synchronous two-shoulder shrug.

"It's being relayed to the Rapid City district office. They know the situation over here best, so it's up to them to decide."

"And you're confident they'll make the right decision?"

"I have been ordered to be confident."

Which was an answer but not a very satisfactory one.

* * *

White Owl obviously managed to pull the right strings, and pretty fast too, judging by the two black SUVs that arrived that afternoon at four o'clock in a medium sized dust cloud at the trading post. Four man in fitted lightweight suits got out of the first one. Two of them entered the store, while the others kept an eye on the surrounding countryside. One returned from the shop, and opened a rear door of the second vehicle. A man dressed in a grey suit got out, accompanied by two obvious subordinates, both armed with attaché cases. The door opener pointed in the right direction and the threesome ambled up the stairs.

They entered through the screen door and encountered me while I was coincidentally reloading the coffee maker. Okay, perhaps not all that coincidentally, I happen to reload coffee makers quite regularly. Ria, who was just adding a dose of info to her tablet at the long table, looked at least as surprised as me. Eddy stuck his still wet head out of the bathroom.

"Mr. and Mrs. Verslooees? Mr. Kamminga?"

I confessed that was us, correcting the pronunciation of my name I had given up days ago.

"James Warren, Assistant United States Attorney."

Really, that's how he said it, capital letters and all. He shook our front paws, returned them, and accepted our invitation to sit down. His two aides were not high ranking enough to be introduced, but they were allowed coffee, a positive sign that all roads to a successful career were still open. While one of the two had a notepad at the ready, the other unfolded a laptop, and Warren began.

"I'm in charge of the Rapid City office, we were informed by special agent White Owl's superiors that something is going on here."

"A kidnapping, a drug gang, yes, I believe that's a reasonable description."

As a good American Warren didn't do sarcasm.

The door opened again, and to my surprise Ankie Schieving, the Postmas' friend, entered. My jaw must have dropped literally, because the others observed me with sincere fascination. Obviously I wasn't missing any fillings, they would have told me, after all we were all at the same side.

Warren gestured to a still vacant chair.

"I believe you've already met? Mrs. Sjeeving was friendly enough to deliver some documents from our mutual acquaintance, Pater."

"You know Pater?"

She shook her head.

"Only vaguely, but he looked me up just before my departure, and asked me to run a few errands for him since I was going here anyhow. Sorry I didn't tell you before, he told me to keep a low profile."

Politely I pretended I believed her, and got another coffee mug for her. Warren continued. He explained what his function entailed, something like a district attorney, only totally different. I was grateful he made that perfectly clear.

"We are now certain the Greek mafia is behind Mrs. Kammingas kidnapping. We have been informed that the organization is being led by a certain Theofanis Kalevras, a former Thessaloniki lawyer."

"A Greek? What is he doing over here?"

"There is a very well organized Greek mafia in this country, with its roots in Philadelphia, but I'm not sure yet if these are a part of that or an independent organization. Anyhow, we assume they will want to use their compatriots' network as their sales channel."

I leaned forward.

"But do you know where they are?"

The American head was shaken.

"I'm sorry to say we don't. Special agent White Owl will have told you already that our position over here is far from optimal."

I could have held a presentation right then and there about how it had come to be like that, but first of all I had one of my temporary cases of civility, and secondly it wouldn't have done any good anyhow, I feared. Quite incorrectly my silence was considered to be an agreement.

"It does have its benefits."

He motioned for his computerized assistant to close his laptop, the other one got the message as well and put down his pen.

"Since we're not here we might decide not to adhere to some of the rules too strictly."

Certainly somebody in Pater's league, that was clear. A warning finger was stuck up in the warm air.

“Do not misunderstand me, I cannot break the law, nor order anybody else to do so. What I can do is agree to a more liberal explanation of the rules, and some reports may be seriously delayed or even disappear because of some clerical error, not on purpose, naturally.”

“Naturally,” I agreed. Ankie nodded as well.

“There is a serious drawback. If we’re not here we cannot fully guarantee your safety.”

I shrugged.

“I’ve been shot at, my best friend’s wife has been kidnapped, how much worse can it get?”

Ria nodded in agreement.

“It’s all the same to me, as long as we get Natasja back safe and sound.”

That there was a serious lack of encouraging official comments was self-evident.

VII

Okay, so we had to come up with a way to trap the gang. Naturally I didn't really like the idea for the three of us to function as bait, but we consulted Jeff Slaughter as well as Billie White Owl after Warren left, and they saw no other options, so Warren did get his way, with us as unhappy participants. My only hope was that this time they wouldn't shoot, after all they needed Eddy alive. My suggestion that Ria would stay behind in the trading post and out of the line of fire was met with a destructive look and carefully chosen accompanying words. Since I had my heart set on staying intact and alive for quite some time longer I asked her in a friendly tone of voice if she happened to feel like coming along. Indeed, she did.

Both Jeff and Billie were brimming with well-meant suggestions which occasionally contradicted each other. I decided to just nod approvingly and follow my own instincts where applicable. Not that this was always that successful, but at least it would be my own decisions, sometimes it might even feel like I could actually influence whatever happened.

It was quiet at the Wounded Knee memorial site when we arrived there. Ria bought a necklace from the poor sod who told us the story of the massacre, a different poor sod than the one who sold me one earlier, and we strolled over to a nearby stand. At a table under an improvised canopy sat a man and a woman with a modest display of dream catchers and jewelry in front of them. Not until we struck up a friendly chat did we notice that Ankie Schieving was hiding under the woman's black hair. Since we didn't know if we were being watched we played along.

She sold us a dream catcher and a decorated miniature drum, and gave a plausibly sounding talk on the symbolism of the colors used. Her dark make-up matched her dyed black hairs perfectly, and somehow she fitted the perceived Native American image better than some Lakota we had seen.

Once our wallets had been skillfully emptied we strolled up the hill. Here as well there were no other tourists in sight. Like during my last visit, two men stepped out of the shadows of the gateway. They welcomed us friendly, and told us the by now well-known history of the cemetery. They seemed to be different dudes from the last time, but I wasn't 100 % certain. Ria bought a necklace from each of them, and a thought crossed my mind that if she went on like this we'd have a lot to explain to customs by the time we got back at Schiphol.

Because we were early and obviously nothing was happening yet I showed Ria the monument. Eddy didn't have a mind to look at the monument right now, though he explained it slightly more colorfully, and remained at the gate.

"They're coming!" he called out suddenly. Quickly we rejoined him, and saw a large black car laboring up the path. In front of the gate but some thirty feet away from it the car stopped. The two front doors swung open, and two Mediterranean types, Greeks perhaps if Warren was right, got out. They tried to do so as unsuspicious as possible, but yet approached us with drawn automatics. Automatically we stepped back a bit, till we were almost at the cemetery gate.

The duo stepped through the gate, and as soon as they saw the guns the two souvenir dudes backed against the wall, their empty hands in full view.

One of the two gunmen took a photograph from his chest pocket, and compared it to Eddy's and my faces.

"You Kamminga?"

Eddy nodded silently.

"Come with us, see woman, see boss."

I looked him in the eye.

"It's all going to be fine, Eddy, you know that."

His expression didn't display a lot of confidence in my words, but he nodded, and stepped forward.

"Come," the spokesman of the duo said.

Ever so slightly insecure Eddy approached them. They turned around, each grabbed him by an arm, and started in the direction of their car. In the meantime they didn't take their eyes or gunsights off us.

All of a sudden somebody called out. From behind the chapel a woman appeared, with a girl of about two years old by the hand.

"Welcome to Wounded Knee!" she yelled from afar, obviously terrified we would leave before she could reach us.

I wasn't the only one distracted, the two guys who were about to abscond with Eddy also looked at her. Automatically their guns also aimed in that direction. That moment was all the two souvenir salesmen at the gate needed. With a few steps they reached the gangsters who after a few karate-like chops against their beefy necks they decided to take naps, quite spontaneously on the dusty path between gate and mass grave.

The woman who had caused the commotion stood there watching, mouth agape, the child pulled tight against her. Without the little one she probably would have taken a runner already, and who could blame her?

Handcuffs clicked around the wrists of the unconscious dudes, and while one of our rescuers kept an eye on them, the other went to the woman. He showed her his empty hands, and addressed her in Lakota. At least, I assumed that's what it was, since I didn't understand him, and it seemed like she did.

Two black SUV's appeared at the gate, and all of a sudden there were another ten men to take control of the prisoners.

Before they left again, one of them took the time to say: "White Owl will call you."

One of the new arrivals got into the gangsterian car, and carefully the caravan descended the narrow and steep track. Ria gave me a puzzled look. Besides the three of us only the woman and her little daughter remained on the sun scorched hill top.

The woman hesitated a moment, then pulled a beadwork necklace from a pocket. Ria bought it.

* * *

The next morning little remained of our victorious mood. Eddy, Jeff, Billie, Ria and me were in the back of Jeff's workshop at a table that had obviously had seen a lot during its long life, mugs of fresh coffee in our respective hands.

The dark mood was caused by a message from Billie that the two Greek prisoners only opened their mouths to ask for their lawyer and the Greek consul. They didn't get to see either, since Billie assured us their paperwork had been misplaced, and would stay so for a while.

"So, we are not a single step closer" I sighed.

"I think so," White Owl answered. "First of all Kalevras is now missing two of his men, and he doesn't know why. They disappeared from the face of the Earth, car and all. That is bound to make him insecure."

Eddy looked sad.

"As long as he's not going to harm Natasja out of insecurity ..."

Billie shook his head.

"No, he won't. He doesn't have a clue what's happened, and he still needs Kamminga. I don't know how long he'll wait for his disciples, but as soon as he gives up, he'll be in contact again."

Billie looked at Jeff.

"Wim told me a lot of people are searching. Any results yet?"

Obviously not, wouldn't we have heard by now? The shaking of Jeff's head confirmed my impression.

"No, nothing yet, but we've fired up the local circuits. There have never been as many people on the lookout as there are now."

"Presuming they're still on the reservation..." Eddy added.

"Our people are still around as well, Eddy," Billie attempted to cheer Eddy up a bit. Eddy nodded in reply, but I could see his heart was not in it.

It was no coincidence my telephone began nagging just as I was bringing my coffee mug to my lips, since that's what I do nearly all the time. I decided to postpone my next sip and to say my name after pushing the green button.

"Why are you endangering Mrs. Kamminga's life? Where are my men??"

Kalevras wasn't talking, he was roaring.

"I don't know what you're talking about, I only know I was standing there for two hours, roasting in the sun on that stinking hill with that damned cemetery. Those men of yours never showed up, maroon! What kind of game are you playing? We are the ones willing to cooperate to get all of this behind us, but then you'll have to work with us! Perhaps next time you should pick men who won't run for the hills! If you ask me they saw what was coming for all of you and picked an easy way out!"

My verbal avalanche temporarily shut Kalevras' mouth.

"If this is a trick, Versloos…"

"Yes, I know the routine," I interrupted him, "you'll start mailing us little bits of Natasja. Don't be an idiot, we were there, and your guys weren't. I suggest you think properly about who you can still trust, if any, before you call me again for a new rendezvous. Oh, and please pick anything but Wounded Knee this time, I really have enough necklaces and dreamcatchers by now."

Without waiting for his reply I disconnected.

"Something like that? I asked White Owl.

"Something like that," he confirmed approvingly.

In the meantime Eddy had promoted himself from fiery red to white hot.

“Wim, I know we have been best friends for a very long time, but if this goes pear shaped, I swear you’re a dead man.”

“Eddy,” I said, “this will work out fine.

It actually sounded like I believed it.

“Let’s go,” Ria suggested, “let’s return to the trading post, we might as well be rested by the time he calls again.”

* * *

It was almost dark when my phone whined for attention again. Jeff Slaughter was so excited I had to keep my electronic chatterbox at some distance from my ear. Eddy and Ria, who were at the table with me about to devour a meal crafted by Susie, looked up expectantly.

“We got them, the bastards!”

Some more exclamations followed, but in the end also a more coherent story.

“My boys talked to everybody they encountered, all over the rez, no results, nothing. Many people already knew by now what it was all about, but nobody had anything new to add. I was beginning to fear they were outside the reservation after all, or perhaps even in Nebraska or as far as Wyoming. But a few minutes ago Frank Shoots Twice called, he knows where they are!”

We learned that Frank came home that evening, and naturally told of the search. Whereupon a nephew, who also lived there, said that he perhaps knew something. He had seen several carloads of strangers at a remote house, and there was a woman staying there as well.

“Did he see her?”

Some discussion at the other side.
"No, but he saw the washing line. There were things hanging there men usually don't wear."
I looked at Eddy.
"An intimate question. What color underwear was Natasja wearing when she was kidnapped?"
The distraught look in Eddy's eyes was temporarily replaced by a dreamy one.
"Red with black lace."
I relayed the information electronically to Jeff.
"Color?" I heard him ask his nephew.
An exchange in Lakota followed at the other side, followed by:
"Red and black."
"Bingo!" I yelled in perfect Lakota, I pride myself in my knowledge of languages. "Where are they?"
"That's the mean bit of the story. They're not on the reservation proper, but just outside. To be precise, you could say they are my next-door neighbors."
Eddy uttered a yell I hadn't thought him capable of. Obviously noisy waters can run deep too.
"Jeff, we'll inform White Owl and his club, if he hasn't been listening along again, and then we'll come to your place. Where do you live?"
"You'll never find it. Let's meet at the gas station."
"We're on our way already.
After a short call to White Owl the three of us ran down the stairs. Before our take-off Ria stuck her head into the store to tell Susie and Andrea, who were quite successfully keeping customers at a distance, that we were going and why.

With an absolute record-breaking speed we blew through Manderson and Wounded Knee, and along Highway 18 towards Pine Ridge. A wild turkey who decided to cross in front of us was only two inches removed from being reduced to a cloud of unattached feathers.

The rare Pine Ridge pedestrians stared in surprise as we raced down the nearly deserted main road at undiminished speed. The single traffic light happened to be green, which probably saved several other road users from the fright of their life.

The by now familiar pick-up was there already, with Jeff leaning against a fender. Billie White Owl was standing there with him, they were talking intently.

They greeted us.

"Let's go along with Jeff right away, so we can see the situation over there for ourselves. I called Warren already, and promised to keep him posted."

In convoy we raced out of town, Billie and us in pursuit of the white pick-up. That wasn't as easy as it sounded, Jeff was well acquainted with both the functioning of the gas pedal as well as the nearly total absence of speed traps. After a few turns we were out of town and could keep an eye on him much easier on the open road.

Suddenly we saw his brake lights flare up, and disappear to the right. Now we bumped along an unpaved drive, passing under a sign with, among other things, a buffalo silhouette, and up a hill. Right next to the road I saw some horse-like shapes as we flashed by, as well as some larger dark shapes that must have been buffalo, I realized.

Jeff's house was of modest size, and neatly maintained. The kitchen we entered was connected with a living room where the main focal point was a gigantic buffalo head over the couch. I'd hate to think what would happen if such a thing would come down while I was peacefully slurping my coffee. On the horns rested a long bent staff, decorated with eagle feathers. I had seen such a thing at the wacipi, leaning against a flag staff, and I presumed it was the local version of a flag or banner.

We avoided all falling head risks because Jeff directed us to the kitchen table while he filled the coffee maker. As the brown gold dripped through the filter he put a dish with odd dry chips-like objects in front of us.

"Go on, try it, real buffalo, you won't find better jerky anywhere."

I had seen some bags labeled "jerky" in the shops here, and Ria had assured me they were slowly appearing in the Netherlands as well, but I hadn't had the faintest idea what it was. Jeff noticed how we three Dutch were looking a bit hesitate at the stuff.

"It's just dried meat, nothing more, nothing less. Stays well for a long time, this has always been one of ways to preserve meat."

I tried a bit, it was delicious! Obviously it had been sliced against the grain because it was very easy to chew.

Billie looked at Jeff.

"Is everything in place?"

A short phone call, and he nodded.

"They are on top of it."

Our inquiring looks went from one to the other.

"We know where Kalevras is, but it might be better if we can lure them out into the open. That's what's in the works now."

That night on nearly every façade, tree or streetlight in Pine Ridge a note appeared:

"Eddy wants a contact. Why didn't anybody show up?"

Many of the town folks must have wondered what the meaning of it was. In the meantime Eddy was chewing his nails while trying to get his phone to ring by the powers of hypnosis.

All of us were sitting at the picnic benches next to Jeff's house, looking absentmindedly at his youth group's teepees, and the brown meadows with horses and indeed buffalo.

Suddenly my cell phone demanded my attention.

"Do you know the gas station at the traffic lights?"

I did indeed, we were there only yesterday.

"Tomorrow morning, nine o'clock. Kamminga will come alone. He'll sit at a table and wait for us. Somebody will come to pick him up. If you plan something else there will be gunfire, and innocent people will die."

"Understood."

"And no more stupid notes!"

The connection was ended. White Owl grinned broadly.

"Wanna bet he'll come himself? By now he doesn't trust anybody anymore."

He looked at Jeff.

"I'll take care of our side, your role is clear?"

"We'll be there."

* * *

It was quiet. Very quiet, Too quiet, perhaps. I feared somebody might notice the lack of traffic since we closed BIA (Bureau of Indian Affairs) highway 32, but hopefully the house where Kalevras and his henchmen were residing was too far removed from the road for them to notice it.

Billie, Jeff, Eddy, Ria and I were laying next to each other in the tall grass on the low ridge separating Jeff's farm from the Kalevras place, a bit over half a mile to the west of us. We were just across the crest so our silhouettes wouldn't show. A few young men of Jeff's acquaintance were laying next to us, or were busy behind us, out of view. Two middle age gents who were introduced to us as veterans each led a group of youngsters. Veterans, I was assured by Jeff, still were highly honored individuals over here in accordance to the warrior tradition, and it showed in the respectful looks in the youngsters' eyes.

At least an hour too early for the appointment a car with two of the Greeks left.

"Care to bet they are going to scout the place, to check for ambushes?" White Owl grinned.

Well, they could scout to their hearts' delight, there was no ambush at the gas station.

"Won't they see the road blocks?"

"There will only be roadworks, they won't see anything out of the ordinary."

And they didn't. Later we learned that first they circled the gas station by car, then again on foot, until they finally sauntered nonchalantly through the whole of the shop and restaurant. Once outside again one of the two made a phone call.

Probably as a result of that call the door of the house opened again. Two dudes came out and each went to a car. They started their engines, and waited. A few minutes later the door opened again. Now another six men came out. One of them was a bit shorter and considerably wider than the others.

"Kalevras," Billie said. He signaled Jeff, who produced a bird sound.

I looked behind me, and saw smoke rise from the other side of the rise. A few buffalo appeared on the top of the hill, to our left, nervously eyeing the smoke behind them.

It took them a while to get moving, and I began to fear that our plan would fail, but suddenly the wind picked up again. The burning grass flamed up fiercely, and the smoke went directly in the direction of the herd. The enormous quadrupeds shook their heads, clawed the parched ground with their hooves, and all of a sudden all of them started running. Nothing could have stopped them anymore, even a gun would have been as effective as a peashooter against a locomotive.

The Greeks were mid-way to their cars when they heard the thunder of the hooves. Stupefied they saw the black rough haired mass storming straight at them. The ground trembled.

One of the man took his gun and fired a few shots. I don't know if he hit anything, but in any case it had no effect. The others, and I recognized Kalevras in that little group, started running to reach the safety of their cars in time.

Some of them made it. He almost made it. But, not quite.

The buffalo herd didn't even slow down but just kept running, up the hill behind the house.

"How do you switch them off again?" I asked Slaughter.

Once more he grinned.

"The boys are already at it to extinguish the fire. A fire truck also arrived. When they notice nothing is burning anymore they'll stop and we can drive them back. They'll have to make a detour, they won't want to pass through the burnt area."

Half a dozen riders were by now following the herd at a respectful distance, but I lost sight of the Wild West show when they disappeared over a rise. In the meantime heavily armed men in black uniforms had appeared to take control of the Greek.

"Come," White Owl said to us, "time to go into the house."

I tried not to look at what remained of Kalevras and two of his men. Ironic, flashed through my mind, that he with his obsessions with beards was beaten by a creature with a rough beard…

A few not totally trampled men got to their feet, and the drivers got out of their cars, all to be greeted by our friends in black.

White Owl entered the house according to the rules, portable cannon in one paw, megaphone in the other, covered by some fellow artillerists.

He roared a message into the seemingly deserted house. If Kalevras had before he left…

But no, the door opened a bit, and somebody waved a white piece of cloth. Billie ordered everybody to come out, hands over their heads. Everybody happened to be exactly one guy, and he wasn't looking overjoyed. He had seen how his boss and some of his colleagues had been buffalodozed, and any possible trace of resistance had disappeared like the proverbial snowball in hell.

Two men pushed him to the ground and adorned him with a generous amount of hardware.

In the meantime Billie cautiously entered the house, followed by two black clad and thoroughly armed colleagues.

Very soon he came out again, and gestured at Eddy and me to come in.

Eddy is even less of a sportsman than I am, but in this race he beat me hands down. Ria jogged after us. Enthusiastic sounds indicated Eddy and Natasja had found each other. Ria and I found them tight in each other's arms in the kitchen. Natasja sobbed as she pulled us into a group hug, as Billie watched with a broad smile on his face.

"You are fine? He didn't harm you in any way?"

Very decidedly she shook her head.

"A few times he tried to pull me on his lap, but I told him I'd scratch out his eyes. Luckily he still needed me."

She looked at the door.

"You did get him, right?"

Billie nodded.

"He won't bother anybody anymore."

She sighed with relief.

Afterwards

"I'm afraid to ask, but what exactly happened yesterday?"

That was Susie, while she was recoffeeing our mugs. We were all assembled around the trusty long table of the bed and breakfast over the trading post's store. Those 'all' were besides Eddy and Natasja and Ria and me Jeff and Billie.

Eddy was about to start when the screen door opened and Ankie Schieving came in, her familiar smile plastered all over her face. The hair dye obviously was of a stubborn variety, she still had black hair.

"Ah, I figured you would all be here."

Susie directed her to an empty chair.

"Coffee for you too?"

Ankie confirmed that she too could not live by tea alone and sat down.

I looked at her.

"To be honest, I'm quite curious."

She giggled.

"So am I, Pater always says."

"May I enquire into your role in all this?"

"You may, that's why I'm here, to give some explanation. I have known Mr. Pater for quite a few years now, I happened to have encountered him because of a previous job. I believe he has people all over the place he can ask once in a while to check into something for him."

Pater as a spider in his web, yes, that did fit as a glove.

"And that's how you happened to be at the Postma place?"

Her head was shaken enthusiastically.

"No, that was an actual coincidence, we've been friends for years already. When I told Pater of us meeting he hatched the idea to send me over here as his FBI liaison, but also to keep an eye on things personally."

"So, no Colorado Buddhist symposium?"

"Sadly, no."

I looked at Eddy.

"Do you start or do I?"

"Sorry, I'm occupied with my coffee."

The maroon…

After I told everything I knew, and Eddy and Natasja had filled in some details, it got very quiet around the table.

"Your buffalo," Eddy asked Jeff suddenly, "are they okay?"

"Oh, they are very sturdy. As are we, we're not called the Tatanka Oyate, the Buffalo Nation, for nothing. One cow was grazed by a bullet, but I doubt she even felt it during all that excitement. I put some ointment on it, she'll be fine."

"Glad to hear that," Eddy said, and the rest of us nodded in agreement.

"Are the Greeks you caught alive talking?"

He nodded.

"They're singing like canaries. It looks like Kalevras came up with this plan all by himself, without any connections with other organizations. Taking those first two prisoner at Wounded Knee really had a great effect, from then on he turned completely paranoid and didn't even trust his own people anymore."

He took a sip.

"I've been involved in some large scale operations, but none as strange as this one."

Everybody could see his point.

"We do strange well," I concluded. That had to sink in for a moment.

"Would you mind very much if we got some peace and quiet now?" Natasja asked.

Everybody nodded. Nobody really believed it. Some people just weren't meant for peace and quiet.

Post scriptum

I won't blame you if you're wondering by now what is fact in this story, and what is fiction, and you're entitled to some background information.

Let's start with what's real. The report of the travels to and in the Pine Ridge Reservation is based on our own personal observations. The Oglala Lakota Sioux over there really are in such a bad situation, unadulterated Third World conditions. The poverty is horrible, many are starving, and in winter the extreme cold takes its toll. Stichting Cosmic Fire Foundation, this book's publisher, is one of the organizations trying to change that. By purchasing this book you've contributed. More contributions are always welcome, by the way.

The trading post, the Kyle College, the Manderson and Sharps Corner stores, the Wounded Knee cemetery have all been described as I remember them, just like the Crazy Horse Memorial and other places mentioned by name. The road Wim was shot at indeed leads through a truly breathtaking landscape, but it has been paved by now.

The wacipi impressions are also based on our own observations, my wife and I attended two.

Various persons in this book really exist, though under different names, and leading much less exiting lives.

Perhaps you noticed that I didn't describe all who were as an Indian or Native American, at most I describe them as "local". I am assuming that all readers understand that the inhabitants of an Indian reservation actually are Indians, so I didn't feel the need to label each individually.

About White Clay: at the moment alcohol sales are suspended, hopefully forever.

Jeff Slaughter's real life version does indeed breed buffalo, but as far as I know he never deployed them as tanks

Billie White Owl as well as his district attorney, James Warren, only exist in my imagination, as does Mike Two Horses.

The gang boss's name, Theofanis Kalevras, was borrowed from a Greek friend of mine, and a former fellow moderator of an internet forum. He assures me that in reality he is not a criminal but a lawyer. Good story, I'd stick to it, you can never tell who will believe you eventually.

Ankie Schieving is a close friend of my wife and me. She is in reality the chairwoman of the Wildervank Buddhist Center, Himalayan Sorig Foundation, and she claims to have no connections with Pater. But then again, she probably would also deny that if it were true, so to be honest we still don't know anything for sure.

The main characters only exist on the paper you're holding now, and that is also where their adventures took place.

I hope this mixture of a real background and a fictitious story was to your liking. I certainly enjoyed writing it.

Oh, and by the way, we did manage to get the stacks of crates and boxes Wim described out of our living room by now…

Gerrit Postma

www.ingramcontent.com/pod-product-compliance
Ingram Content Group UK Ltd.
Pitfield, Milton Keynes, MK11 3LW, UK
UKHW020127250726
13967UKWH00002B/522